THE SILENT SOCIETY

Printed in Australia
Cover design by Shawline Publishing Group Pty Ltd
Images in this book are copyright approved for Shawline Publishing Group Pty Ltd
Illustrations within this book are copyright approved for Shawline Publishing Group Pty Ltd

First Printing: May 2023

Shawline Publishing Group Pty Ltd
www.shawlinepublishing.com.au

Paperback ISBN 978-1-9229-9305-2
eBook ISBN 978-1-9229-9311-3

Distributed by Shawline Distribution and Lightningsource Global

A catalogue record for this work is available from the National Library of Australia

More great Shawline titles can be found here:

New titles also available through Books@Home Pty Ltd.
Subscribe today - www.booksathome.com.au

THE SILENT SOCIETY

RICH LARSEN

Solvitur ambulando

CHAPTER 1

Light filtered through cracks in the blinds, letting piercing rays of early morning glow through the bedroom window. It cast a beam directly onto the face of Jenson, who reluctantly opened the one eye that wasn't submerged in the pillow. He blinked a few times to gain focus of his surroundings and brushed away the loose strands of sandy hair caught in his eyelashes. His mouth was dry and his body ached but that was nothing unusual. The youthful days of springing out of bed each morning had long passed. He wiped his eyes and gradually spread his hands across the roughness of his unshaven cheeks. He felt twice the forty-two years he supposedly was. Years of field work and travel around the globe had taken its toll. It was a privileged position to be in, he had to remind himself. To wear yourself down with something you love whilst being surrounded by the wonder and beauty of the natural world. Something he never got tired of was the peaceful feeling of waking to the sounds of forest birdsong, rain on a tin roof and water eddying over river rock. The feeling of being at home in beautiful bushland would always be the fuel to his fire and the reason he woke up each day. His travels had taken him all over the world but there was nothing quite like the familiarity of his local mountain range. He knew every twist and turn of the river that jutted its way through the valley, every nook and cranny where fish liked to hide and the best time of day to catch them.

Despite his rough appearance, sometimes blunt attitude and remote living quarters, Dr Jenson Ryder was an intelligent and thoughtful man. His research across the preceding decades had led him to become a senior research fellow at a leading university that was renowned for their work in epidemiology and biological anthropology. Despite his success, he never pushed for status within the scientific community and instead longed for knowledge and understanding of the unknown. His passions really remained out of the lab and in the natural wilderness where there was still so much to be explored. In a way, he had two lives. A professional life that contained him to a stale white laboratory and office space, illuminated by the harsh frosted light of fluorescent globes. It was a good job and one that he enjoyed but in the end, it was a means for him to live the life he always dreamed of as a boy. A life connected closely to his natural environment by hiking, fishing and exploring. This was the element of his life that fuelled him and gave him purpose and meaning. Without it, he was lost, lonely and depressed. He had firsthand experience of what occurred when you isolate a human being to the confines of a concreted world. The echoes of foreign, intrusive sounds, smells and sights day after day drained on his psyche and eventually led to full-blown depression. There was a time when he tried to convince himself that it was the life that everyone had to live, or perhaps that's what his ex-wife had tried to convince him of.

Jenson dragged himself to the bathroom where he turned the faucets of the shower and soaked himself in steaming warm water. Silky pure liquid ran through his hair and across his skin, quelling the goosebumps brought on by the early autumn air. Jenson's time in the outdoors gave his skin a weathered appearance that aged him further than his forty-two years. Despite this, his face retained a youthful healthiness. His academic life was yet to sterilise his semblance. He insisted on wearing his hair long, the sandy strands hanging over his forehead and ears, framing his deep blue eyes. His body was thin and wiry, yet strong and durable, trained by the ebbs and flows of life. Were it not for the woollen dress coat he often wore to work, he could easily be mistaken for someone at home in Hawaii chasing waves.

He lived in a wooden cottage that rested on the banks of the Capertree

River, a couple of hours west of the main city and on the border of a vast and dense National Park. At this stage of the morning, a gentle stream of wood smoke spiralled from the chimney, which floated gently across the valley and down the river. The early glow of sunlight that had previously woken him had yet to melt a thin layer of frost that blanketed the grounds surrounding the house. Droplets of dew clung to eucalyptus trees and the sound of whip birds echoed out through the bushland. For Jenson, it was a piece of paradise where he could escape the noise of the modern world. When he wasn't at the office or his laboratory, he could be found fly-fishing and canoeing the local rivers and hiking through the National Park. It was like being transported back into another era, to a place where time was irrelevant and the trivialities of the world seemed so opaque and insignificant. It was a place where you could think deeper about the things that mattered or not think at all; it was up to you where you let your mind wander.

The whistle of the kettle broke Jenson from his daydream, his blue eyes peacefully staring out the window of the kitchen. He loved the way the early morning fog lingered in the troughs of the land and across the riverbeds, hiding all but the tips of surrounding trees. He poured the boiling water to brew a mug of tea and watched as the steam swirled mesmerisingly up into the room. He stood in the front doorway, feeling the warmth of the house on his back and the brisk touch of dawn air on his face. The hot tea melted down his throat and warmed him from the inside out.

There was a time when Jenson was able to share such moments with his wife. However, the strain of constant travel by chasing research opportunities in far-flung corners of the globe had placed immeasurable strain on his relationship. Her constant disdain for anything outside of the city had been the breaking point in the end. They simply wanted other things out of life. They had different priorities and couldn't find the compromise to make them stay together. It had been a difficult few years following his divorce but Jenson finally felt as though he was getting his life back to a peaceful place where he could move on with the things he loved. He was a man that valued time alone with merely the presence of the natural world. Sasha, his ex-wife, on the other hand, had found the idea of isolation almost repulsive. In the post-mortem following the divorce, he wondered how he had not seen that trait in her from the beginning. Hindsight is a wonderful thing though, and in hindsight, his divorce was probably the best thing that could've happened. He'd been able to move permanently into the place at Capertree and set up a life had always wanted, not the way 'it was supposed to be'. Conformity was never one of Jenson's strong suits. Although he missed Sasha, his life now was much simpler and far more relaxed. As he soaked in the rising warmth of the morning sun finishing his cup of tea, he finally realised that he was reversing the damage. He felt whole again, almost new.

Jenson looked down at his wristwatch and realised he would be running late again if he didn't get a move on. He downed the meagre remnants of what was in his mug, brushed his teeth and dashed for the car. The satisfying crunch of gravel under the wheels soon subsided to a smooth sound of tarmac and before long the bushland gave way to open farmland and transitioned further to urban sprawl. The drive to the office was never his favourite. Coming home was the highlight. Whether it be a beautiful clear sunset or a thundery day with pouring rain, there was never a moment when the drive out of the city didn't leave a satisfied feeling deep in Jenson's gut.

CHAPTER 2

Jenson was climbing the several flights of stairs on the way up to his office when he was stopped by his administrative assistant. Her face was flushed and a concerned furrowed brow immediately raised his suspicions, as she was generally a calm and controlled person. She informed Jenson that he had multiple messages from a place called the Centre for Intelligence and National Security (CINS) and required him to call urgently. Jenson had to think twice about what he had just heard. The words national security echoed in his head as he was handed their contact information on a small piece of white office paper.

'Did they say what they wanted?' Jenson asked, looking slightly confused.

'No. They just said it was a matter of national security so they had to speak directly to you on a secure line.'

'National security. They used the words *national security*?'

'Yes. And to call them urgently,' she reiterated.

'Thank you,' Jenson replied, still holding the square piece of paper in his hand. 'Can you block my schedule for the morning then? No calls. No meetings.'

Jenson stood in the hallway outside his office for a moment. The fluorescent lights humming above him mirrored the static he felt in his brain. Why on Earth would CINS want him to call them… urgently? *National security*; the words rang through his head again. He broke the thought and hurriedly placed his briefcase on his desk and dialled the number scribbled on the piece of paper he held in a slightly sweaty hand. A low raspy voice answered.

'Dr Ryder, thank you for calling me back so soon.'

Jenson stuttered for a second at the rapid acknowledgement of his phone call. How did he know who was on the other end of the line?

'Uh, not a problem. Sorry, who am I speaking with?'

'My apologies, Dr Ryder. My name is Hiram Nebu. I am the director of CINS. I assume your assistant filled you in on why we're speaking today?'

'Well, no. Not exactly. I was informed there was an issue of national security that you needed my help with. That's all I know. And before you start, I have no idea what issue of such a scale I could help you with. You do realise I am just a human ecologist who works at a university?' Jenson's voice became unexpectedly hurried and he found himself suddenly flustered.

'I'll stop you right there, Dr Ryder.'

'Please, call me Jenson.'

'Very well. I'll get straight to the point, Jenson. Our data are showing an acute rise in the number cases of a disease that has severe morbidities associated with it. We do not yet know the pathophysiology of this disease. The first reported case was a little over six months ago but has been exponentially rising ever since. We were alerted to the situation when we received notification from hospitals and mental health clinicians across the country that they were being inundated with patients at an unprecedented rate. We are yet to determine the exact cause and have not found a medical professional who has come across such an illness before.'

'What sort of symptoms are we talking about here?' Jenson asked, suddenly feeling slightly more intrigued and less worried he'd been the subject of an elaborate hoax.

'The symptoms are wide-ranging and vary in severity. However, we are predominantly seeing a massive spike in the number of patients accessing help for feelings of depression and suicide coupled with extreme lethargy, pain and an inability to speak.'

'They're mute?' Jenson quickly interjected.

'In some cases, yes. In most, all we are seeing is a few words here and there and nothing remotely coherent.'

'And the depression? Are there any similarities in cases that you've observed so far?'

'It's difficult to tell due to the incoherence and uncommunicativeness of patients. This is where we need your assistance. Further analysis of these patients is desperately needed from the ecological level; from the ground up. We need to get into the field and see what's going on. We need to understand how this illness is manifesting and what can be done to prevent it and ideally cure it as well.'

A silent pause in the conversation left Jenson with the realisation of what this man was asking him. The enormity of it suddenly struck him. His heart raced and his mind flickered through scenarios like the reel of an old movie.

'And this is what you want my help with?'

'That is right, Jenson. We have done our research and clearly see that you are the premier researcher in this field. We want you to head the research into this crisis.'

Jenson slowly sat down in his office chair and contemplated the scenario for a while. It was a lot to take in first thing on a Monday morning. Could he just drop everything and start working for some strange organisation? How did he even know the person on the other end of this line was telling the truth? He wanted to be back at the house, in the forest without a care in the world. His mind searched for an easy option. He wanted someone to walk through the door and tell him it was a false alarm and he could get back to his day. It had started so peacefully, yet here he sat.

'Are you still there, Jenson?' Hiram asked, breaking the silence Jenson had left hanging while taking it all in.

'Uh, yes, I'm still here. Sorry. I'm just… just… I'm…'

'I know it's a strange situation I've put you in here. But you must understand that this is something we need to get on top of as soon as possible. If we're going to do that, I firmly believe you are the best person for the job.'

'I'd like to set up a preliminary meeting to go through the basics in person and gain a better understanding of what's going on here. I need to assure myself of that before I commit to anything more.'

'Of course, I understand. I'll have a helicopter pick you up within the hour. Just bring the bare essentials. We'll take care of the rest.'

'Did you say a helicopter?' Jenson replied in a slightly bemused tone.

'That's right, Dr Ryder. Be ready in thirty minutes. Someone will collect you.'

Jenson slowly placed the phone down on the receiver and rested his hands on the desk. He stood motionless for some time, his face depicting the epitome of confusion. He then snapped into action, packing some items into his briefcase and frantically scurrying about his office, wondering how best to prepare for the meeting, and being summoned by a helicopter.

CHAPTER 3

Lights flashed at random intervals and a mind-numbing static pulsated through Sasha's brain. It hurt to blink. In fact, it hurt to move any part of her body. Her limbs fired explosive shots of pain with every attempted muscle contraction. Sweat beaded on her forehead, arms and chest, making her cold and clammy. A mental a physical exhaustion overwhelmed her to a level she had never experienced before. Sleep was hard to come by with the constant chatter of electric impulses speeding recklessly through her central nervous system. *This is it,* she thought. *This is the end.*

Sasha's state had been declining over the past few weeks but she was now reaching breaking point. She tried going to the doctor to explain her symptoms but could hardly get a word out over the noise within her mind. From what she recalled of the consultation, she sat there for the entire time almost mute, straining to get her point across. All the while, her mind was screaming out in agony trying to escape a living hell. The last thing she recalled was the doctor escorting her out to the waiting room where she battled in distress back to her car. She had no idea how she drove home again. And now here she lay on her sofa, almost waiting to die. She couldn't move to call for help, to get something to eat or drink or even yell out in hope that a neighbour would come to her aid. Her eyes displayed a fear that reflected a helpless animal that would soon be prey. She tried to close them, relax and forget what was happening but it was impossible to shut down the pain. *This is it; this is the end.*

CHAPTER 4

The roar of the rotors chopped violently through the air as it descended on the sporting ground near Jenson's office. The sleek, black helicopter gracefully touched solid ground and a suited man scurried out to greet Jenson amongst the noise and gale generated by the machine. His hair and tie blew sporadically as he approached, causing him to shield his face from the occasional gust.

'Dr Ryder, thank you for coming. Please follow me and we'll get underway.'

Jenson followed as he was told and scrambled aboard the helicopter alongside the man. He gave the pilot the signal to take off and the engine surged to life once again. Before long they were climbing steeply into the air with Jenson's office shrinking by the second until it was a distant speck among the cityscape.

Jenson tried to avoid cities where possible but could never find the capability to remove his connection to them altogether. He looked down from the helicopter with a mixture of despair and disgust as they rolled over the sprawling skyline of high-rise apartments and offices. There was something unsettling about the view from above. Without the noise and hustle of being on the ground, it created a third-person perspective of an environment that was rarely viewed in such a way. The lack of colour was demoralising and the ant-like structures that were actually cars, buses and trucks looked absurd for some reason.

The man he had followed onto the helicopter handed him a headpiece to allow communication which broke his tangential thoughts.

'Dr Ryder, can you hear me?' he said, pointing to the earpiece on his headset. Jenson gave a nod and a thumbs up.

'Yes, loud and clear,' he replied to test the system.

'My name is Abel. It's my job to oversee your activities during your project with CINS. Anything you need, you come to me. I will be travelling with you for the most part and reporting back to Hiram. Should you choose to come aboard, we'll be working closely with each other to uncover as much as possible about the sudden surge in this illness we're observing. I must stress that you cannot talk to anyone else about your work with us. The public cannot get a hold of this or all hell will break loose. The press will have a field day and there will be widespread panic and unrest across the world.'

Jenson nodded in submission, still unsure entirely what was happening and who he was with. The stakes seemed to be escalating by the second.

'This is an international problem?' he finally replied, trying to keep up.

'It looks that way. Our contacts in Europe are observing spikes in illnesses with very similar symptoms. We're working closely with our counterparts to contain the situation and keep everything under wraps. I cannot stress enough how important your confidentiality is on this matter, Dr Ryder.'

Jenson sat back for a moment to take all this new information in. From what seemed to be a normal Monday morning, he was suddenly hurtling through the sky in a private helicopter to work on a global health issue of top-secret importance. It was difficult to comprehend at this stage, so he tried to distract himself by focusing on the task at hand. If there was even a remote possibility that he could help find a solution to this problem, he wanted to try. He had always been a determined person and flourished in the face of adversity. It's what he loved about nature. It was constantly adapting and changing to be the best it could be. Even when disaster struck, there was a means of repair and regeneration; be it bushfires, floods or volcanic eruptions.

He thought back to his homestead at Capertree and the attachment he had developed to his surroundings. The peacefulness and tranquillity washed over him like diving under a wave in the ocean. He felt calm, relaxed and focused. Within moments, his brow relaxed to reveal a steeliness within his dark blue eyes. His jawline tensed momentarily, sharpening his muscular face.

'I'm going to have to take your phone, Dr Ryder.' Abel's voice interrupted. 'Just to make sure we are completely secure. As I said, this cannot be leaked out into the public, no matter the circumstance.'

Jenson reached into his trouser pockets, pulled out his phone and placed it in Abel's prying hands. The gravity of the situation was beginning to take form and Jenson realised it may be some time before he returned to his regular life.

CHAPTER 5

A sudden crash of thunder woke Sasha from a delirious state on her sofa. The room lit up with the subsequent lightning and her eyes ached as she tried helplessly to orient herself. Still in agony and unable to comprehend where she was or why she was feeling so awful, she painfully levered her sweat-soaked body into a more upright position. There was a lamp on the table beside her which she reached to switch on. Nothing happened. The sound of her breath was heavy in her head with every laboured effort as she looked around the room for any other signs of light. It was then she realised she was sitting in complete darkness in her home, all alone. Her breathing got faster and heavier until it overwhelmed any other sound around her. *Calm down. Think. Take a step back and think.* Another clap of thunder reverberated through the foundations of the house, sending her mind into overdrive once more. Her eyes darted around the pitch-black room. Strands of wet hair caught in her eyelashes. *Calm down and think.* It was then Sasha realised the power had to be out. There were no illuminated clocks, no standby power lights on, nothing at all. She tried to drag herself off the sofa to investigate further but sudden shockwaves of pain pulsated through her body, knocking her down into a foetal position. Rain battered the windows as she slowly drifted out of consciousness again, her hair covering her eyes from the intermittent strikes of lightning.

CHAPTER 6

The rotors of the helicopter slowed and the sound of the engine died with them as Abel and Jenson walked across the concreted roof of an inner-city skyscraper. Cloudy skies painted a bleak picture of the surrounding city, which to Jenson really did resemble a concrete jungle. Boxes of light illuminated sections of buildings as office workers busily went about their day, oblivious to what was occurring. The sound of trains, buses, cars and motorbikes echoed from the streets below creating a sense of urgency and unrest, even from high above where Jenson observed.

'Right this way, Dr Ryder,' Abel interrupted, gesturing for Jenson to enter the building from a solid steel doorway on the rooftop. Jenson sped into a trot to catch up and entered a dark doorway that led to steep, scarcely lit concreted stairs. *Where the bloody hell are they taking me?* Jenson began to think this was suddenly an elaborate kidnapping plot.

'My apologies for the dim lighting. Be sure to take care down the stairs. We had to take precautions on the location of headquarters for this project. As I mentioned, we need complete secrecy to avoid public panic.'

At the base of the stairs was a large red metal door that was sheathed by an old-fashioned elevator slide. Abel drew back the metal slides to reveal the door and placed his hand on a palm reader beside it. A green light flashed and the reader beeped twice, prompting the door to unlock and slowly slide open. The scene before Jenson at that moment was something of a dream, something only seen in movies with undercover agents and intelligence programs that only a select few were aware of. A pristine white room was occupied with glass touchscreen monitors meters wide and equally as tall. A small group of people were congregated around one, moving items around a world map like the puck on an air hockey table. A large circular table in the centre of the room housed a hologram of Earth, which was suspended in the air, slowly rotating. There were no windows to be seen, creating the feeling of being in an underground bunker, despite standing at the top of one of the tallest buildings in the area.

A tall dark-skinned man approached Jenson and Abel. Like everyone else, he was dressed in a black suit and tie with black shoes that reflected the glimmers of light bouncing off the white walls and ceiling. He had a thin build with long limbs. His face was distinctive with narrow eyes, a wide nose and a square jaw. Jenson estimated he was a similar age to him, perhaps in his early to mid-forties and was completely bald. He stepped towards Jenson with an outstretched hand.

'Dr Ryder, sorry, Jenson. My name is Hiram, we spoke on the phone not long ago. It's great to finally meet you and thank you for coming. We are in desperate need of answers and could do with someone of your expertise.'

Still overwhelmed by his surroundings, Jenson slowly reached out to shake Hiram's firm hand, all the while scanning the room.

'You have met my assistant, Abel. Let me introduce you to the other members of the team.'

Hiram's long strides escorted Jenson effortlessly across the white tiles to the screen where two other people were standing. They were still looking at the map of the globe and touching certain countries and regions creating fluctuations in the bar graphs that were scattered across the screen. One of them was an elderly man with wispy grey hair and thick black-framed glasses. He was small in stature with a slight hunch, making it difficult for him to look towards the top of the screen in front of them. Beside him was a woman in her early thirties with long dark hair and a striking face adorned with brilliant green eyes.

'Emerson and Nya.' The pair turned from the screen to face Hiram and Jenson. 'This is Dr Jenson Ryder. He will be our field officer on this project, should he choose to come aboard.'

The two of them smiled and nodded courteously.

'Jenson, I'd like to introduce you to our two lead analysts, Professor Emerson Grant and Dr Nya Olsen. They will be both assisting you in your research into the prevalence and incidence of these cases. With any luck, we can get on top of this sooner rather than later.'

'It's a pleasure to meet you,' Jenson replied, shaking both their hands politely. He noted the discrepancy in the feel of Emerson and Nya's hands in his, the latter providing a soft yet stable grasp over Jenson's weathered palm.

'We've heard great things about your work, Dr Ryder,' Nya said, engaging in conversation that was designed to fill the empty spaces around the awkward combination of people who had never met and were somehow to come together to solve an international crisis.

'Please, Jenson is fine. And thank you for the kind words. I am surprised anyone pays much attention to the work we do. May I ask where you work?'

'Both Emerson and I work alongside Hiram at CINS. Emerson is the lead analyst in the environmental department and I coordinate the sociological department. The two of us saw this rising trend over the passing months and were finding it hard to believe our data. We collaborated with one another to make sure what we were calculating was indeed what was occurring in the real world. Once we had, we knew drastic action was required.' Nya's voice projected a distinctly international accent that Jenson could not place. Part English, Scandinavian and American all scrambled into one. Emerson, he had noted, was yet to say a word and stood formerly to attention while Hiram, Nya and he conversed about the situation at hand. He nodded occasionally and muttered words of agreement, his bushy eyebrows shadowing the upper rim of his glasses.

'So this is the team that will save the world,' Jenson said with a bantering smile, trying to ease the sterility of the situation. 'It's not quite *The Avengers* but I think we'll be a productive unit.'

The others smiled with him and with that, Hiram led Jenson to his office where he offered him a seat and something to drink.

'Jenson, I want to give you a rundown of what we expect from you on this project and what you can expect from me and the other members of the team.'

Jenson nodded with expectation. After all, this is what he was here for. What he was about to hear would make or break his decision; although in the back of his mind, he believed he had already committed to it the moment he set foot on the helicopter. Something of a cunning plan by Hiram to gloss the situation up a little more.

Hiram outlined what the next few months of Jenson's life would be like. It involved extensive travel and with that, the ability to remain inconspicuous as to why he was travelling far and wide. As Abel had deliberately informed him already, it was paramount to keep the public in the dark to prevent widespread panic. His confiscated phone and ban on communication with friends and family were a testament to this.

Jenson's primary goal was to find out what was happening at a deeper level physiologically across differing populations around the world. Investigation on those with and without the illness was required. He would travel with state-of-the-art equipment that allowed brain activity to be monitored in real time, allowing him to isolate specific sections of the nervous system, if any, that were responsible for the onset and development of the disease.

'We originally developed this technology for military purposes but like so many inventions that start out that way, it is now being used in the health and medical field as well.' Hiram's tense jawline and terse way of speaking made him the stereotypically high-strung manager of an organisation such as CINS. Jenson began to wonder what the military were doing with such technologies and arrived at a fairly grim conclusion, so decided not to pursue the topic in conversation.

Hiram brought up a world map on the large window screen in his office, which was coloured with varying depths of red.

'Here we have the known prevalence of the disease so far. The darker the colour, the more cases in the area. As you can see'—Hiram indicated with a laser pointer—'the hardest hit regions seem to be large cities.' Hiram zoomed into central Asia, highlighting the significant proportion of cases in Beijing, Hong Kong and Tokyo. 'Your first assignment is to head to Tokyo, the area with the most reported cases in the world. We need to gain an understanding of the pathology of the disease: who it's infecting; are they young, old, male, female, construction workers or office dwellers? You catch my drift.'

Abel swiftly and unobtrusively entered the room and handed Hiram a piece of paper.

'Thank you.' Hiram looked more concerned than before. He walked over to his office chair and cloaked himself in his suit jacket, buttoning it up with swagger and efficiency. 'I'm sorry, Jenson, but I must leave you for now. I must brief the nation's leaders and subsequent advisors. Abel will see you to your quarters and equip you with everything you need for your journey.' With that, he exited his office, leaving Jenson to absorb everything that had just occurred in the past couple of hours.

'This way, Dr Ryder.'

CHAPTER 7

The morning song of a magpie woke Sasha. She was still on the couch and in the same clothes from yesterday as far as she could remember. The pungent, sweet smell of sweat hung in the room as she leveraged herself upright. Her hair felt thick with perspiration and stuck to her forehead, neck and ears. Her mouth was painfully dry and her head ached with a pain akin to nothing she had experienced before. She got up and walked to the kitchen, opened the fridge and grabbed a bottle of water. It was gone in a matter of seconds as her parched lips and tongue soaked up the liquid. She refilled it and finished it again and then realised something was not right. Firstly, how did she get to the kitchen? Yesterday she could barely move a muscle without piercing shots of pain pulsing through her body. And secondly, she noted that the water from the fridge was no colder than that out of the tap. She walked back to the fridge and opened it. No light. Everything was warm. It was then she remembered the storm last night. *The power must be still down*, she thought to herself, and then noticed none of the clocks in the house were working. She had no indication of what day or time it was, how long she had been out for or how long had the power been out for.

The magpie squawked again outside the kitchen window. Sasha pulled the curtains back to cast bright sunshine across the room, which at first made her eyes ache but once she adjusted to the light it was like her mind had rebooted and the neural connections to her muscles were mobilised again. Looking out across the yard, she revelled in the green grass that somehow seemed more vivid than she could ever remember. Her neighbour was busy filling buckets with ice in a frantic manner. Opening the door out to the back garden, Sasha felt the warmth of the sun on the exposed areas of her skin. It rejuvenated her to an extent until she peered down across the backyard to neighbouring houses. Everyone looked a mess. Distant shouts echoed down the street and there was the ring of sirens from every direction. It was then Sasha began to really think she had been out for longer than just a day.

Speaking to her neighbour, she discovered the power had been down for the past week due to a heavy storm that obliterated the network of power lines in the area. They were the worst hit and were the only area to still be without power. It was, according to him, 'a bloody disgrace in this day and age'. All Sasha could think about was how much better she felt. She assumed she hadn't eaten much within the past week, yet she felt surprisingly spritely after being outside for a time, letting the warmth of the sun recharge her. She was by no means fully healthy again but she was mobile and in considerably less pain than she last recalled. Time still seemed to progress slower than usual and she found it difficult to express herself when speaking with her neighbours. Her fatigue seemed to be more mental than anything though, which confused her, given the battering her body had taken with very little nourishment of late. There was a lingering black cloud that hung over her head that caused a cloudiness in her judgement and mood.

Suddenly, a cascade of noise swept through the street. As Sasha looked up, there was a wave of lights switching on in the houses around her. Cheers of rejoice echoed around the neighbourhood as people relished in the restoration of normality. In a strange way, Sasha almost found it sad.

CHAPTER 8

The flight to Tokyo continued Jenson's run of firsts for the day, as he switched his usual cramped economy seat for the luxuries of a private charter in a small jet – all without paying a cent. A seat that fully reclined to a bed that was laden with soft blankets was something so foreign on an aeroplane that he almost forgot that he was thousands of metres in the air. Not to mention the in-flight bar service. The view down into Tokyo looked that little bit better with a scotch in hand.

'This is how you usually travel?' Jenson asked Abel as he inspected every nook and cranny of the aircraft like a small boy exploring a new house.

Abel looked far less enthusiastic and requested that he and Jenson sit down to liaise about the protocols they needed to follow once on the ground in Tokyo.

After touching down, Jenson was escorted through the airport to a private car and whisked away to a building not far from the city centre. He was advised that these were his quarters for the next few days where he would both live and conduct the necessary research. The room was small but not cramped and contained a bedroom, a small kitchen and living area, and a separate room for work. It was this area that amazed Jenson the most. The room was filled with state-of-the-art medical equipment that would allow real-time analysis out in the field. He could simply go out and begin researching, it was that simple. There was no red tape, no boundaries on what he could or couldn't do. All he had to do was update Hiram and the team at Headquarters as to his progress and any findings he needed in-depth assessment of. The candy store seemed to be getting larger by the moment.

Jenson whipped the curtains back from the large solitary window in his high-rise apartment to reveal a cityscape littered with artificial light. There were millions of streetlights, headlights from cars, lights from billboards, lights from buildings. It was the middle of the night but there was enough luminescence to see clearly around the surrounding streets and beyond. Jenson had to remind himself he was now in one of the most densely populated cities in the entire world. It wasn't just the light that astounded him, it was the noise as well. He guessed he was about one hundred metres in the air, yet he could hear everything from the surge of engines accelerating from traffic lights to the shouts of pedestrians walking the footpaths below. There was an incessant humming of mechanical generated noise that was inescapable, even when all the doors and windows were closed.

Sitting in the corner chair with a freshly brewed cup of tea, Jenson reflected on the whirlwind past twenty-four hours. He thought back to his morning at the house in Capertree and what had transpired since then. He had no idea that the day would lead him to Tokyo on the hunt for evidence of a mysterious illness. The tea soothed his throat, which was dry from the flight, and he finally began to relax and not think for a while. He decided tomorrow would be a better time to investigate his field equipment and develop the best strategy to collect data. The steam from the cup swirled gently up to his face, transporting the calming scent to his nose. A warm sense of calm and relaxation ran through his veins and for the first time in over a day, Jenson took it all in.

CHAPTER 9

The usual sounds of birdsong and wind rushing through eucalypt trees were replaced by the honking of horns and clutter of city life. It was an unusual awakening for Jenson, who still sat slumped in the chair with his mug from the night before resting on his lap. His mouth was dry and skin taught from the flight. He looked around the room, slightly dazed, before comprehending where he was. He gathered himself for a moment before inching his tired and aching body from the chair. A clouded light pierced through a gap in the blinds. Jenson walked over and opened them to reveal a cityscape draped in fog, or smog, he couldn't tell the difference.

After stepping out of the shower and inspecting the range of gear he had to take out in the field, Jenson heard a knock at the door. He answered, still dressed in his robe, and found Abel standing before him.

'I see you have settled into your new lodgings, Dr Ryder,' he said, looking up and down at Jenson's regal hotel appearance.

Jenson, not one for self-indulgence, felt rather embarrassed but was more excited about the prospect of utilising his new toys for the purpose of ground-breaking research. He ushered Abel through the door, after which he was handed an envelope.

'These are your specific instructions. What to assess, particular regions of interest, et cetera, et cetera. These have come from Headquarters in collaboration with the Japanese government. Nya and Emerson have worked out the sample sizes needed as well. All you need to do is collect the data and report back.'

'It's that simple?' Jenson retorted, feeling as though his role in this was being underestimated by this man standing before him that he hardly knew. He did always seem to be impeccably dressed and punctual though, which demanded respect to some level. He had a ruthless efficiency to him, much like Hiram. It was probably why he had hired him as his assistant. There was a hint of father and son relationship between the two of them.

'It's that simple,' Abel replied. 'I'll see myself out. Your next schedule is also enclosed. I'll see you before we leave.'

Before we leave. They had been in Tokyo for less than 24 hours and already he was talking about the next assignment. The door closed and Jenson unravelled the letter containing all the details he required. He was to collect 1000 real-time cerebral magnetic resonance imaging (rtMRI) scans from specific regions of the city and observe these populations as they interact with the environment around them. Jenson was to be the mind that knew the workings of the diseased mind, an intellect that was able to spot the nuances of this pathology and collect the raw data accordingly.

While reading through the letter laying out his instructions, Jenson once more felt the weight of the assignment he'd agreed to take on. The task now seemed more daunting than ever.

CHAPTER 10

The streets of Tokyo were bustling with people scurrying their way through the early morning air, albeit laced with industrial fumes. It was the beginning of spring and there should've been a vibrancy in the step of those roaming the city. Instead, what Jenson encountered was as staggering to him as anything he had seen. Neon signs battled against the sunlight that punctured through concrete crevasses created by surrounding skyscrapers. Cherry blossoms were beginning their bloom after a winter hibernation, creating a sweet smell in the midst of a polluted city. It was these pockets of the natural world that fascinated Jenson. The construction of a human world had strangled the expansion of natural landscapes, yet it continued to leak through as many holes and gaps as possible. Inch by inch, tree roots cracked the concrete above them, while moss and lichen clung to pipes and city walls, creeping to wherever moisture would allow them.

It wasn't just the natural world that had been strangled. Like the glassy eyes of fish caught in a net, the people Jenson encountered on his first day on the ground looked resigned to an inexorable decline. Headphones shut down interactions with each other and their surroundings, perhaps in an effort to suppress any pain. Their eyes were fixated on nothing in particular to avoid eye contact with others. Most looked to their phones or tablets, navigating by following the feet of those in front of them. The procession was an eerie one to witness as an outsider.

After half an hour of observation, Jenson thought he'd seen enough. It was time for him to collect some hard data to back up what his eyes had just witnessed and what his anecdotal evidence reiterated. He found an elevated position that was relatively secluded and removed a small device from his bag. From a distance of about twenty metres, he was able to focus in on individual subjects and obtain cerebral readings from the state-of-the-art rtMRI machine. It was much like operating a speed gun for tracking speeding motorists. After some time, Jenson was able to quickly and efficiently gain the data required to ascertain what was occurring at the neurological level. The numbers were rolling in after an hour or so and he was soon up to his required 1000 samples that Headquarters requested. Physiological data followed with more instruments that he had never laid eyes on before but soon mastered. All the while, he was documenting what he observed to provide some subjective nuances to the raw data that was spewing from the technical work.

Back at the hotel, Jenson trawled through his notes to find common threads that he had identified. The physiological data seemed to reveal a new set of stories that were hard to believe at first impression. The human body was an incredible thing, able to adapt to any array of situations that placed homeostasis in jeopardy. What became obvious that evening in his hotel room was that several biological systems were operating under severe duress. Elevations in cardiovascular and respiratory markers were present, but what was most surprising was the fluctuations in normal hormonal levels. Jenson could hardly believe the numbers he was recording. Cortisol, ghrelin, leptin, testosterone – all seemed to be way out of normal ranges. He made notes furiously as he waded through the data, while simultaneously sending it off to Headquarters for further analysis.

There seemed to be equal weighting between men and women, something that wasn't uncommon for a lot of central nervous system pathologies. However, further observation revealed that there was a disproportionate number of people under fifty years of age who were displaying abnormalities. While he was purely estimating a subject's age upon surveillance, there was a strong enough correlation between age and physical observation that he thought it was worth further analysis. From first impressions, there wasn't too much he could identify but he emailed the data through to Emerson and Nya back at Headquarters with the subject line 'Hereditary?'

CHAPTER 11

Jenson found it hard to sleep that night. Images of the thousands of people, emotionless and limp, clouded his thoughts as he stared at the apartment ceiling. After seeing the effects of the disease firsthand and on such a large scale, he began to wonder what it was he could do to curtail this rising beast. He thought back to the years of fieldwork he previously completed – all the research findings that he had published and it suddenly seemed a little abstract and pointless. If the intelligence that CINS had gathered was correct, this disease would surface in every living human within the year. He wasn't sure if something could be done in that timeframe that would elucidate any significant change.

Back at Headquarters, Emerson and Nya scrolled through the raw data that Jenson had sent through overnight. There was little doubt that the younger generation seemed to be more susceptible to the illness as he had suggested.

'Either that or they present their symptoms earlier. Or perhaps even have worse symptoms than older individuals?' Nya suggested to Emerson, who sat poised on his leather back chair deep in thought, his eyebrows muffling the glimmer of surrounding lights from his eyes.

'Like the common cold or flu?'

'Exactly. Think about the majority of communicable illnesses and diseases that have presented around the world in human history. Who's usually worse affected? The young, extremely old or the sick. This could be exactly the same.'

'I'm not convinced,' Emerson retorted. 'There's something more to this than meets the eye. It's not presenting in a way that a communicable disease does. It hasn't spread in the manner that an outbreak of influenza has.' Emerson signalled to the graphs and maps scattered around them with historical data. 'Take the H1N1 2009 avian outbreak throughout Mexico and the US. There's a distinct pattern emerging as the disease spreads throughout the population and we're able to reverse engineer this model to locate the source. Now take a look at the model we have for this current illness.'

The movements on the screen in front of the pair were distinctly different and they replayed it over and over with an overlay of the 2009 outbreak. It was clear there was a discrepancy and they were no closer to understanding what they were dealing with.

'What about Jenson's suggestion?' Remarked Nya.

'That it's hereditary? I'm not so sure but he's the one on the ground. It could be a possibility but I find it hard to reach that conclusion given the data we've collected so far.' Emerson sat for a moment and rubbed his eyes beneath his glasses. He then looked at Nya. 'If Tokyo is the worst hit, perhaps we need to get some data from areas where there haven't been any reported cases yet.'

'To support the case that it's hereditary?'

'Simply to flip the coin and get some corresponding data sets. Instead of asking why something is the way it is, perhaps we need to ask why it's not.'

Nya sat, deep in thought at the profound comment. Her smooth, soft skin slightly crinkled at her cheeks as she debated the idea.

'I'll call Hiram and get him to send the request through to Abel and Jenson,' she finally said.

CHAPTER 12

With power restored to the neighbourhood, Sasha went about getting on with her daily life and tried to piece together the puzzle of her mystery illness. She barely remembered a thing from the time she was sick, apart from being in immense physical and psychological distress. She still had little concept of the time that passed since her sudden demise and was too proud to probe her neighbours if they had spotted her recently and what condition she had been in. Some colour had returned to her face but her usually vibrant blue eyes were dull and lifeless. Plus, she stank. She couldn't believe the stench that was emanating from her body. At first, she thought it was something in the house and then realised it was her. A shower was in order.

The hot water felt calm and soothing across her grimy skin as it washed away the build-up of sweat-soaked sickness. She let the water run through her hair and soak her bones in an effort to rid herself of lethargy and depression. She had never taken a longer shower in her life and eventually, the water ran cold and woke her up from a state of heat-induced lethargy.

As she put on a fresh set of clothes and continued her detective work of what had happened over the previous week, she heard a shallow knock at her front door. It was her neighbour from a few doors down, Michelle. They both looked at each other and immediately saw the grief-stricken appearance on each other's faces.

'It happened to you too, didn't it?' Michelle finally said, breaking the silence.

'You can't remember what happened either?' Sasha's hair was still dripping from the shower and her skin was flushed from the heat.

'Bits and pieces but it's hazy at best.'

Sasha stepped aside from the door and gestured for her to enter.

'Come in,' she said with a flick of her head.

The two of them discussed what had happened and shared eerily similar stories of their recent days. Fits of extreme pain, headaches and a depression so deep that it created crevasses in the mind that were irrevocably haunting.

'It was only when the power was down that I started to recover,' Michelle said, almost like a confession to a priest. Sasha nodded in agreement, as she stared blankly at the kitchen table they sat at.

They both agreed to keep an eye out for one another over the coming days and exchanged phone numbers. After seeing her out, Sasha immediately thought of someone to call, someone who she thought could explain what was happening. She scrolled through her contacts and pressed the name of Jenson Ryder. The phone rang out again and again. She must've tried half a dozen times or more before relenting and leaving a voicemail.

'Jenson, it's me… Sasha. I know…' She paused with a heavy weight of hesitation. 'I know we haven't spoken for some time but I have something I need to ask you. Can you call me as soon as you get this? I wouldn't call if it wasn't important.'

She hung up and slumped into a chair as she felt another wave of lethargy overcome her. The memories of her time with Jenson overwhelmed her mind. None of them seemed to make sense though; she couldn't comprehend the emotions that were bouncing around between her head and heart. Finally, she relented to the urge of sleep and for a moment she was able to relax.

CHAPTER 13

Abel and Jenson met at a café down the road from their apartment to discuss the next stage of the mission. The place was full to the brim in the early morning rush but just as Jenson had witnessed yesterday, there was a futility and dampness that resonated through the room. It was like being at a concert but everyone was listening to the band through headphones. There was little interaction between people and there was a hollowness in everyone's eyes. It was unlike anything Jenson could rationally explain or had ever witnessed before. When somebody looked at you, there was no recognition, just a vacant stare that seemed to look straight through you.

'I've received word from Hiram that we're to go to the forests of the Congo for our next phase of data collection. We've collected data from the worst-hit area on the map. It's now time to go to the other end of the spectrum.'

Jenson's first reaction was excitement. He had often longed to go to the remote areas of Africa but had never had the opportunity. There remained tribes hidden within the dense bushland of the Congo that the outside world had yet to discover. Hunter gatherers who lived as hominid ancestors had for thousands of years prior. Explorers often ventured down tributaries of the Amazon to find such remote people and places but for Jenson, it was the Congo that held the pedestal. Abel continued to talk about the logistical challenges of reaching the place of interest to which Jenson nodded and agreed, all the while thinking of fulfilling a boyhood dream.

'Does that all make sense, Dr Ryder?' Abel finally said.

Jenson was bemused by Abel's incessant formality of calling him Dr Ryder. He'd given up asking him to call him by his first name and accepted that he was more machine than man, something that Hiram appreciated no doubt.

'Ready when you are.'

CHAPTER 14

After a stop-over in Dubai, which entailed Jenson's inaugural visit to a first-class airport lounge, he and Abel were soon jetting high above the Red Sea on their way to the Democratic Republic of Congo. The journey was far from settled with huge turbulence buffeting the shell of the plane like a paper kite.

'The DRC has the highest frequency of thunderstorms in the world. Hence the turbulence,' Jenson said casually, trying to lighten the tense atmosphere of the cabin.

Abel was far from impressed, gripping tightly to his armchair, the whites of his knuckles rising with each passing minute. All the while, the world's second-largest rainforest was below them, gurgling and alive with a landscape that graced the earth during the Jurassic period. Fed by the East African Lakes and Albertine Rift Mountains, the Congo River and surrounding rainforests was as wild a place that anyone could go in this day and age. It was Jenson's job to find a remote tribe there and gather the valuable data and intelligence that could help alleviate all those suffering from a silent illness. As the plane touched down on the runway, Abel expelled a sigh of relief and his pained face gave way to a nervous smile.

'Never again, Dr Ryder. Never again,' was all he could say as they collected their belongings from the stowage bins above.

A wall of heat and humidity greeted them as they exited the cabin and walked to the small airport base across the tarmac. The sun was setting but the heat remained and radiated up from the black surface beneath them. Jenson had no idea how Abel was coping in a suit and tie. His hair remained slicked to the side and somehow the hectic schedule and demanding environment hadn't seemed to ruffle his appearance at all. Not even a 'near death experience', as he had put it, could place a crease in his shirt. Jenson on the other hand was embracing the time out of his office and jumped at the opportunity to dress down. He wore blue shorts and a white shirt with the sleeves rolled halfway up his forearms and loosely buttoned across his wiry athletic frame. A pair of black reading glasses sat atop the bridge of his nose, the only item that resembled his academic life. In this moment, Jenson was truly a man of two worlds. The academic intellectual who explored off the beaten path.

It was late by the time the pair reached their hotel. Abel had argued with the reception staff as to the condition of his room, while Jenson was amazed such incredible facilities were available in this part of the world. He was glad they didn't stay in Kinshasa, the capital of the country. It seemed like an oppressive place in more ways than one. Decrepit concrete structures rose from the ground in an ad-hoc manner, stifling its eleven million inhabitants by trapping the heat of the day. Instead, they had travelled on a short flight from the capital to Lisala, which was nestled on the northern banks of the Congo River. From what Jenson had read, the town had a hostile past, witnessing the site of many conflicts, including World War II. As a result, many parts of the town were permanently without connection to basic services such as water, electricity and sewage. It was a stark contrast to the neon lights and technologically driven society that he witnessed in Tokyo a little more than a day ago. Despite the challenging circumstances, the city had produced a hotel of exemplary quality. Jenson's room was open air, allowing the scents of the river and forest to mingle through the windows. By this stage of the night, cicadas were in full voice and the rustles of the dense foliage a few hundred metres away were offset by the sound of the Congo and Tshuapa rivers conglomerating into one.

It was almost as if he had been transported to a rainforest version of his house in the hills of Capertree. He placed his glasses on the bedside table and sat wearily on the mattress, shuffling his shoes off one by one to stretch his toes. The creaks and cracks of his joints reminded him of his age. He slumped back on the bed to try and filter the noise from his brain. For some reason, he thought of his ex-wife, something he had not done in distant memory. He had well and truly moved on from the relationship and had flourished both professionally and personally since their split. All he could see when he shut his eyes was her face, framed by her light brown hair and marked with vibrant blue eyes that could see straight to your soul. He found it odd the way the mind operated in times of stress.

The phone Jenson was supplied with back at Headquarters binged and lit up with the notification of a new message. Emerson and Nya, with the assistance of Hiram, had identified the area to which Jenson was to travel. His plans were laid out in an itinerary, which began at first light tomorrow morning. *Saving humanity from a pandemic is taxing work.*

He had barely placed his feet on the DRC and he was already assigned a tight schedule of data collection. Abel was to stay behind and coordinate proceedings and arrange the next leg of their journey. He would be travelling with the assistance of a guide on a barge down the Congo in search of the native tribal group known as the Bayaka, a nomadic Mbenga pygmy group scattered throughout the Congo. They spoke their own language and were one of a select group of indigenous tribal populations to be listed in the Masterpieces of the Oral and Intangible Heritage of Humanity by UNESCO. Their society and culture were on the brink of extinction at the time of listing, but select groups remained throughout the densely forested Congo Basin. For the time being, it remained relatively untouched by Western influence. He placed the phone beside him on the bed and closed his eyes. *Was this the expedition to reveal the attack point of this insidious disease?* His thoughts gradually allowed him to drift off and get some sleep before embarking on what would be his most important work to date.

When the alarm woke Jenson from a fitful sleep, he felt as though he barely drifted off. The sounds of the morning felt unnatural after crossing so many time zones. He'd lost track of what time it was back home and thought it better to forget about it anyway. He had a job to do and the weight of expectation and anticipation of getting underway was enough to raise himself from the bed and shuffle to the shower. The water was far from cool with the outside sun already baking the pipes. The humidity only compounded Jenson's confusion and lethargy. He felt like he was swimming through the air as he walked down to the dock where the barge and his guide were patiently waiting in the glow of the morning sun. He shielded his eyes from the reflection of the river as he walked to the banks to see a short stocky man jump effortlessly off the barge to the jetty. He greeted Jenson with a broad white-toothed smile that radiated from his matte-black skin.

'Dr Ryder, hello,' he said in a thick accent that exuded a friendliness that could only be found when travelling this far from home. 'My name is Kofi. I will be taking you down the river in search of what you are looking for.'

'You know what we're looking for?' Jenson replied inquisitively.

'The Bayaka people. But not just any Bayaka man. The Bayaka that nobody knows about,' he said with an air of mischievousness to his voice. 'But me, I know the Bayaka better than anyone around here.'

'And why is that?' Jenson probed.

'I am Bayaka!' Kofi replied with a sense of pride.

Jenson was surprised that Headquarters had revealed anything about the trip to a civilian but then again, he needed to know what to look for if they were ever going to find the data they required.

'So you know this river well then?' Jenson probed as he scanned around the banks, looking at the eddying current of murky water.

'This river is my home. It has brought me life and will be here for far longer than I will be. The river has my respect and when you respect the river it will give you life.'

Jenson nodded and threw his small rucksack onto the barge. It contained only the bare essentials; there would be no room for extraneous luxuries on this voyage. 'Let's get to it then, shall we?'

CHAPTER 15

Hiram's voice was calm and assertive as he addressed the room. For most, it was an idle Tuesday afternoon where the majority of the world's population were going about their business. For a select few within the World Health Organisation (WHO) and associated parties, however, the discussion was far from idle. The disease was spreading faster than the models predicted and to add further difficulty, the models of geographical spread they had created were not accurate either. Instead, what the healthy population were faced with was a waiting game. It was the type of anticipation akin to watching prey being hunted. The danger was palpable, yet there was no way of knowing where it was coming from. It left some in stagnation, unable to move in a world careering into chaos. Others were frantic, panicked by the threat that hung over their shoulders.

As Hiram spoke, those around the room listened intently, some with translation devices fitted to their ears. His tone was firm, yet clear and understanding. Delegates from around the globe gathered tightly around a wooden table to discuss the strategies moving forward. The disease, now referred to as SK01 (silent killer strain 1), was far-reaching and non-discriminatory. In fact, as Hiram eluded to, it appeared the wealthier regions of Europe, Asia and America were the hardest hit.

'I currently have a team of the brightest minds working towards ascertaining the origin and cause of this disease. We have people in the field who are collecting data on those affected and while the analysis of our data is in its infancy, I can assure you that we are progressing.'

Hiram's words were far from comforting but his manner and his tone demanded respect. His thin, focused eyes met each and every other person in the room to relay his confidence to them. At this point, he knew that it wasn't a matter of how he felt but a matter of how he made others feel. He needed those in the room to be at their best and his attitude could make or break that.

After speaking for some time, he was asked how close he believed a cure was.

'... or do you think this is beyond reach in the near future and we need a management strategy rather than focusing on a cure at this point in time?' The man speaking was from Germany and explained that his research team had been all but demolished through the wave of SK01. 'They are still alive but I do not know for how much longer. Like the rest of these cases, they are weak. Not just in the body but in the mind as well. They cannot speak, they cannot care for themselves. I fear that if we do not isolate the spread, before too long we will not have the people to work on this. We need to isolate the healthy so we have a hope of finding something down the track.'

Hiram paused for a moment to assess the question. It was certainly a point well-made but he knew deep down that his team were capable of finding something, and soon.

'I understand your frustration,' Hiram began, his jaw tense and chest tall. 'However, what we have seen from our predictive models thus far is that we cannot accurately ascertain the spread of SK01. If we place all our efforts into containing this disease, we may lose our chance to find the cure while at the same time, fail to contain it.'

The room fell silent and the eyes of the table drifted from Hiram to the German representative. He nodded with a melancholic acceptance as his eyes shifted their gaze to the papers in front of him. Hiram was right; they had failed to work out the basic epidemiology of the disease let alone track its progress and spread. Their only chance of preventing a global collapse was to go all in. Like the bluffing poker player, they had to pool their resources to find out as much as possible on how SK01 developed, spread and thrived in the population.

Hiram unbuttoned his suit jacket, sat down in his chair and entwined his fingers on the desk. At this stage, he wasn't sure if he had convinced those in the room that his approach was the way forward. Other national delegates were discussing amongst themselves, no doubt about the claims he had just made and his proposals. Glances in his direction gave little indication as to the feel of the room; however, there had been an air of apprehension since the meeting had begun. If he was honest, Hiram thought it more to be a feeling of fear and panic than anything else. It was strange what happened to even the most competent and capable people when fear entered the equation. He wasn't sure if *he* was scared, or whether he had convinced his own mind that the team he assembled would carry out their duties and provide a solution.

'I think we have heard enough for today.' The Chairman of the committee finally spoke to quieten the unrest around the room. 'We have heard from various nations today, all of whom are acting with the world's best interests at heart. We have experts in the field and at various locations globally that are working on this issue. As Hiram has highlighted to us all just now, I think the best way to proceed is to tackle this head-on. We can no longer rely on containment and maintenance measures to buy time and gather resources. We simply cannot continue down that path.' Every set of eyes was fixated on the Chairman and his deliberations as he continued to weigh up the options before them. 'We will meet again in a fortnight to discuss progress. In the meantime, please continue to report as per usual protocol. That is all for today, thank you for your time and patience. We *will* get to the bottom of this.'

We will get to the bottom of this. The words echoed through Hiram's mind as he gathered his possessions and exited the building. He knew a facade when he saw one; he'd just pulled one up himself.

CHAPTER 16

Jenson and Kofi gently drifted down the Congo, surrounded by an array of green that was more diverse than Jenson had ever witnessed. He never knew there was so much variation in the colour until now. From the light sandy green of grasses to the deep, rich hue of palms and lily pads, it was almost as though a new colour wheel could be invented just by travelling through the region. The pair had been on the river for two days and were well into the wilderness of the Congo Basin. The sights, smells and sounds of civilisation were a distant memory and instead were replaced by the calls of forest birds and the rustling of tree canopies and foliage. Despite being confined to a 3x2 metre barge for the majority of the day, Jenson found the experience quite relaxing. He was able to read and journal at his leisure while taking in the majestic beauty and ruggedness of the environment as they travelled. He and Kofi had developed an understanding of each other quickly in their short time together. He was not a talkative person and neither was Jenson. They both thrived on the absence of human noise and only spoke when necessary. It was also integral to maintain focus on the river ahead to scout for potential dangers. Fallen trees, rapids, territorial hippos and crocodiles meant that this was no place for an idle and ignorant human being. Vigilance was key and chatting away for the sake of removing the air of awkward silence could be the distraction that brought them undone.

'Jenson,' Kofi whispered over the idle hum of the barge. 'Did you hear that?'

Jenson looked inquisitively over his shoulder at Kofi standing on the stern, crouched in mid-action with his head still straining to listen. 'No. What did you hear?'

There was a shallow thud on the side of the boat that caught the attention of both of them at once. *Thwump*. Again. Jenson gently rose from his seat and stepped nervously over to the edge of the barge where the sound was emanating from. *Thwump*. He crouched down to investigate and just as Kofi was about to warn him of getting too close to the edge, a wave of white water consumed half of the barge and brought Jenson crashing into the river.

'Jenson!' Kofi yelled as he disappeared under the sudden vacuum of whitewash.

It then dawned on him what had been knocking on the side of their vessel. With Jenson out of sight, all Kofi could see was the unmistakable dark grey balloon of an adult hippo careering towards him. Creating a wake similar to that of a jet boat, the hippo was not in a mood for negotiation and was determined to see Kofi topple off into the river as well. It rammed the side of the barge repeatedly in an effort to do so but Kofi somehow hung on. He looked around desperately to see if Jenson had surfaced but couldn't see him. The barge had been reoriented to face towards the river bank and was heading for the eastern side as the hippo came for them again. Blow after blow, the barge hurtled amongst a cacophony of hippo, water, metal and desperate human beings. Kofi's forearms burned as he struggled to grip whatever he could to stay on board, all the while frantically searching for a sign that Jenson was still alive. Minutes passed as the barge was seamlessly ping-ponged around the river; then there was silence. The water settled and the thrashing noise of metal and animal subsided to leave Kofi face up with one hand gripping the tiller. He gradually got up, wary that round two may come at any moment. Scanning the surrounding waters for Jenson, there was still nothing to be seen. The gut-wrenching thought of failing his mission was beginning to dawn on him. He was entrusted the life of this man and after just two days he would have to travel back to Lisala with his head bowed in shame and sorrow. He shouted Jenson's name but all he got was the empty silent air. Not even the call of birds or the hum of daytime insects could be heard, just his own heartbeat and breath as his head swivelled anxiously in search of his travel companion.

After what seemed like an eternity, Kofi finally spotted a figure on the banks of the river. Drenched and dishevelled, Jenson revealed more of a water rat than a human being but there was something more pressing at hand. Just metres away from where Jenson lay, the hippo remained in constant surveillance with its body half submerged and eyes fixated on any movement from its imposter. Kofi, in a desperate act with little resources at his disposal, began to shout and bang on the side of the barge to detract attention away from a helpless Jenson. He wasn't sure if Jenson was even alive. He hadn't seen him move and was too far away to see the rise and fall of his chest to indicate he was breathing. The hippo responded to Kofi's distraction and was soon fixated on the barge.

As it approached in a wake of river water, Kofi jumped off the barge and bolted for the side of the river. He stayed underwater for as long as possible to reduce any unnecessary splashing that may attract the hippo away from the barge. He reached the edge of the river and quickly ran towards Jenson. Without thought, he picked his limp body up underneath his armpits and dragged him as far away from the river bank as possible. After fifty metres of struggle, dragging a dead weight through forest scrub and over tree roots, Kofi finally collapsed in exhaustion. He could hear the hippo continue to maul the barge out on the river and thought they were now far enough away to be out of danger. Still panting, he clambered to his knees and rested his ear over Jenson's mouth. He could hear and feel the slightest of murmurs and see his chest move occasionally. He was alive but only just. With limited medical knowledge, Kofi began compressions on Jenson's chest in an effort to kick-start his breathing. After what seemed like minutes, he could not see any improvement in Jenson's state and was beginning to panic. The forest floor was damp with leaf litter and he was covered in mud and dripping wet. A constant hum of insects and bird calls emanating from all corners of the jungle clouded Kofi's thinking and created a restriction in his own breathing. He was becoming dizzy, his vision was clouded and started to wheeze.

Just moments later, Kofi heard the relieving sound of Jenson cough and splutter as he leveraged himself up onto his elbows and crawled on his side. His face gained some colour, even if it was coated in dirt and leaves from the forest floor.

'I hate hippos,' Jenson wheezed as he looked up at Kofi with a sly grin. With that, Kofi's broad white smile emerged from underneath his mud-stained face.

'I don't think they like you either!'

CHAPTER 17

Sasha woke to what was becoming a familiar scene. Her head was aching, the house was a mess and she could barely remember what had happened in the preceding hours or maybe even days. There seemed to be a constant hum resonating through her body. It wasn't the typical temporary tinnitus that she had after coming out of a noisy room, but something much deeper. It was as though her soul was reverberating. She could barely speak, let alone walk. The terror of what had happened just over a week ago seemed to be returning. She picked up her phone to see if Jenson had returned her call. She somehow remembered that she'd left him multiple messages, although nothing showed up on her phone from what she could see in the darkness of her bedroom. Her despondency deepened as she placed the phone back on the mattress beside her with the signature click of locking the device.

Sasha decided to visit her neighbour, Michelle. In part, it was to check up on her but also to see if there was anything she had discovered about this mystery illness that was going around. When she arrived, she knocked on the door only to find it creak open. An echo of unfamiliar voices bounced through the house and there was a staleness hanging in the air that was hard to place. It was akin to the smell of an old refrigerator that had been sitting unused for months. She called out to see if anyone was home, but the only reply was that of the television. She searched around for the remote to turn it off when she was suddenly alerted to what was being reported on the screen. *Millions disabled as mystery illness sweeps the globe*, read the text at the bottom of the screen. A news anchor with a concerned look on her face was interviewing a medical professional.

At this stage, we think this is a new strain of the common cold or flu and we encourage people to rest and stay at home if they believe they are infected. We want to reduce the spread of the virus as much as possible.

Sasha zoned out as she stared at the screen and slowly processed what she had just heard. It certainly didn't feel like a cold or flu to her. None of the symptoms seemed to replicate those of a common cold. There was no sore throat or runny nose, just an overwhelming lethargy and an unfamiliar feeling in her mind that was like nothing else she had ever experienced. She turned the TV off and continued to look around the house for Michelle, calling out her name intermittently. She was just about to say her name again when she passed a small room off to the side of the house where she saw Michelle laying lifeless on a chair in the corner. There was a blanket loosely draped over her body and her limbs drooped off the sides. Sasha stood in horror at the doorway, completely frozen with a mixture of fear, trepidation and panic. She gradually approached the lifeless body, her feet creaking the floorboards beneath her as she inched closer. Her face was pale and clammy and the underside of her eyes was dark and hollow. Sasha placed her fingers on Michelle's neck to search for a pulse. She was still warm and she could sense a faint breath exiting from her half-open mouth and eventually found a weak pulse. Relief swept over her as she placed her hand on Michelle's shoulder and gently shook her.

'Michelle. Michelle,' Sasha quietly said as she knelt beside her.

She barely moved despite Sasha's constant calls for her to wake up.

'Michelle, you need to wake up now. How long has it been since you've eaten or had anything to drink?'

Her sunken eyes eventually opened and blearily looked over to meet Sasha's. She tried to talk but nothing came out, so she closed her eyes again and sighed.

CHAPTER 18

With their barge smashed to pieces by a rogue hippo, Kofi and Jenson began walking downstream. Kofi had managed to salvage most of their equipment by throwing it into the river as he jumped off. They'd found it a few hundred metres away where the echoes of the hippo could still be heard, its ferocious attack continuing in a territorial battle. Travelling by foot through the jungle floor was painstakingly slow, with their average speed measured more accurately in hours per kilometre rather than kilometres per hour. The two of them weren't quite prepared to invent a makeshift canoe after earlier events. For now, they were content to battle their way through the dense green foliage and avoid disgruntled wildlife.

'Any idea how far away we are from the nearest Bayaka tribe?' Jenson queried as he grappled with a twisting vine that was blocking their route.

'Close. Maybe two days walk from here. Quicker by the river though.'

'You don't say.'

A gentle rain began to hit the forest floor, adding to their already saturated bodies. For most, this situation would've spelled disaster but for Jenson, he was right where he wanted to be. There were no office blocks, road noise or email notifications to impede his thoughts. Even the scents of the tree canopy drifted down and calmed his mind.

'There's probably only a couple of hours of daylight left so we should start to look for somewhere to sleep,' Kofi chimed in after he realised the ridiculousness of his previous comment.

'Let's try and find somewhere away from the crocs and hippos, shall we?' Jenson said, looking over his shoulder to stir Kofi.

Cicadas continued to vibrate the air around them as Jenson and Kofi set up a makeshift camp next to the buttress of a tree. Vines and foliage hung low to the ground, providing some shelter from an inevitable monsoonal downpour. Frogs and peepers echoed calls beneath the damp leaf litter while a curious python swirled its way around a tree branch overhead. Jenson pulled his supplies from the pack he was carrying and boiled some water for tea. The remaining food supplies were beginning to run low, so he hoped Kofi's prediction of finding the Bayaka was correct. They could barely afford to wander, aimless and starving, in search of this mysterious tribe while the world waited for them to find a breakthrough on SK01. They lit a small fire and stared into the flickering flames as the forest around them drew ever darker. They were able to dry some of the clothing and gear and slowly the wounds of the hippo encounter began to subside.

As morning broke, Jenson and Kofi battered their way through to the edge of the river to re-evaluate their surroundings. It was beginning to run quickly with rapids forming at regular intervals. The morning light reflected a mist that hung loosely a few metres above the surface and created a fresh scent in the air. There was nothing quite like the smell of morning air in the wilderness, Jenson thought.

'We should be fine following the river for another day,' Kofi instructed as he surveyed the land before them. 'There is a ridge a few kilometres downstream that we will need to cross. From there, we follow a small tributary which will lead us to the Bayaka.'

Jenson nodded and with a swing of his machete, began to follow the current. He had the hopes of billions resting on the findings of this expedition and time was of the essence. He began to think about those back home and all over the world that were suffering. There would be people close to him that would be gradually dwindling into a state of semi-coma, unable to move or speak to relay their distress. With each person he thought of, he methodically swung the machete, almost in a therapeutic way to rid himself of the negativity. He knew there was no point dwelling on the 'what-ifs', as his best hope of helping them was to do his job and get back to Abel. It was hard to keep his mind from wandering, though. Once again, out of nowhere, Sasha entered his thoughts and he began to think about how she was coping. Was she affected? Did she need help?

'The world needs help,' Jenson muttered under his breath.

Over the course of the day, Kofi and Jenson intermittently exchanged conversation as they rested between the battles of finding their way through the jungle. Jenson was curious to know how a Bayaka tribesman came to live away from his people and create a life for himself in a foreign town.

'It was never meant to be that way.' Kofi gradually spoke as Jenson quizzed him over a papaya they had pulled from a nearby tree.

He felt the sweet flesh and juice rejuvenating his earlier sorrows and physical fatigue.

'Bayaka are a proud people and I did not live up to those standards for a time. As punishment, I was exiled and forced to regain the trust of my community. I found my way to Lisala and began to learn English with the hope that I could teach it to them when I returned. At first, they were reluctant and saw my actions as further insult to my heritage and the Bayaka way. They wanted to remain independent of the stories they heard from the outside world. They were convinced that they would be better off without the influence of others. After all, they have existed this way for thousands of years.' Kofi paused and looked contemplatively at the ground in front of him as he finished the last of the papaya. His eyes grew narrow and his usual vibrant smile had long dissipated. 'I understood their reasoning but my actions were in good nature. I wanted to help and I wanted to rejoin my people. For now, there is nothing more I can do but service their needs by providing any resources they need and can't obtain.'

'Like what?' Jenson probed further, his interest spiking.

'Basic supplies for hunting and building. Rope, metal and hessian are the main things I bring. It helps them without impacting too much on their traditions.'

'They're your traditions too.' There was a pause in the conversation before Jenson finally had to say something more. 'It sounds as though they're taking advantage of you.' He paused and took a moment to assess Kofi's reaction. 'Think about it. You say they want to remain isolated from the outside world and your actions went against that when you went to Lisala?'

Kofi nodded in regret.

'Yet they're now using you as an errand boy to get the supplies they need to make their lives that little bit easier.'

There was a silence that pierced through the mid-afternoon hum of cicadas. Suddenly the humidity seemed to rise and their surroundings became more claustrophobic.

'We should get moving,' Kofi finally said. 'We have limited daylight left and need to find camp for the night.'

Jenson shouldered his pack after stuffing away his supplies and began the steady grind downstream once more. Kofi's limber and sinewy body had already cut a path ahead but could barely be seen through the tangle of vines and shadows of the jungle floor. There was nothing he could do to take back the words about Kofi's place in the Bayaka tribe. He wasn't sure that he would, even if he could. Instead of the melancholy of Sasha's wellbeing hanging over his head, Jenson now had the guilt of shaming his new friend and travelling companion by casting the realisation that he was being used by his own people, that perhaps there would never be a chance for him to redeem himself from his past actions, whatever they were. He began to wonder what it could've been that had resulted in his exile in the first place. There would be no use in continuing to probe further to find out now; the damage had already been done. Trudging forward, Jenson knew there would be limited sleep for him tonight. Despite his fatigue stretching deep into his bones, he knew his mind would rouse any chance of recovery. He was angry at himself for allowing the outside world to penetrate such a wild and beautiful place. The human mind could be the basis of incredible angst if left uncontrolled.

CHAPTER 19

News reports on every station were now latching onto the growing spread of a mystery illness sweeping the world. The TV at Headquarters showed a map of the known cases reported so far, reportedly sourced from the World Health Organisation. A concerned reporter repeated news that had been on a loop for the best part of 24 hours about the new strain of cold and flu sweeping the world. Hiram sat in his office and sighed. For the first time in his professional career, he felt as though he had no control over the situation. The sound of the TV was muffled by rattling thoughts in his head as he pondered what the next move should be. He had always prided himself on competency and the ability to handle even the toughest of circumstances. As he reflected on the current standing of SK01, he realised that this was now hanging in the balance and in the control of officers in the field, such as Jenson.

A knock at his door broke him from a tunnel of thought. It was Nya, who looked equally as tired and concerned about the current state of affairs. Her dark brown hair was tied back in a ponytail, revealing the soft features of her face. Her deep brown eyes conveyed a sense of desperation as she approached Hiram's desk and placed a document in front of him.

'What's this?' he enquired, as he opened the folder tentatively.

'It's the latest projections based on current figures. Emerson and I put it together yesterday while you were away.'

Hiram perused through the contents of the file, his face barely flinching as he scanned the documents.

'Worse than we thought. Although, we knew it would be worse than we thought. So how do you want to phrase this to the WHO?'

'Well, we warned them that this was unlike anything we'd seen before.'

'I don't think that's going to cut it.'

'My thinking is that we need to reiterate the point that SK01 is not spreading in a normal fashion. We've overlayed the progression to that of every major outbreak since records began and it shows no similarity to them.'

'Nya, we need answers at this stage, not excuses.'

'I know, that's exactly my point. What we're looking for isn't a typical virus. We need to start looking at other options. We've been tracking this for months now and come up with next to nothing. What more can we do with our current approach? I think it's time we changed tack.'

Hiram's jawline tightened as he continued to look through the contents of what Nya had just delivered. He was feeding off her anxiety, sensing her discomfort at having to break such dour news.

'You're right,' he suddenly uttered after a period of intense silence. 'If we're going to have any chance of getting ahead of this, we need another route.'

Nya let out a relieved sigh. 'We need that data from Jenson. Any updates?'

'Nothing further to report, unfortunately. I spoke to Abel yesterday but he hasn't had contact with Jenson since he left in search of the Bayaka.'

The hum of the TV continued over Nya's shoulder as Hiram looked up at her from his desk.

'That will be all, thank you, Nya.'

As she went back to her desk, Hiram picked up the phone and dialled Abel who remained in Lisala to oversee the on-the-ground workings of Jenson's expedition. The faint dial tone was interrupted by Abel's familiar voice.

'Hiram,' he responded in military fashion.

'My apologies for interrupting your sleep. Can you update me on the situation? Any word from Dr Ryder?'

'Nothing, sir. I lost contact not long after he departed. The isolation of the place makes it difficult to obtain contact with any consistency.'

'Understood. Send through any updates immediately. We are on the precipice. We need something to grab hold of back here.'

'Sir.'

The line went dead and Hiram was left with his own words ringing in his head. *We're on the precipice.* He placed the phone gently back down on the receiver and considered his next move. He had to have something tangible between now and a field report, he just wasn't sure what that was.

CHAPTER 20

The smouldering ashes of the campfire glowed sporadically in the morning air as dying swirls of smoke lifted through the jungle canopy. Birds sang out from all corners, busy in their morning routines and avoiding the caucus of chimpanzees that rattled through the branches. For once it wasn't raining and Jenson was able to wake to dry clothing, something that felt almost luxurious. He quenched his parched mouth and gradually rose to the usual creaks and groans of his ageing joints. Kofi remained asleep by the other side of the fire. So as not to disturb him, Jenson decided to take a quick trip to the river to wash the embedded grime from his body and survey the day ahead. The river continued to run quickly with rapids carving out deep sections of rock and land as it winded through the forest. Reeds blanketed the far side of the river, making it difficult for Jenson to see across and assess what lay beyond. The ridge Kofi had spoken of lay before them and he wondered with a boyish excitement what his first encounter with the Bayaka would be like. He hoped that yesterday's despondent mood following their conversation would dissipate once they were hot on the heels of the tribe.

After splashing some water across his weather-beaten and unshaven cheeks, Jenson made his way back to camp through the dense foliage and vines. Kofi was awake and tending to the fire in preparation to boil water for breakfast. They were down to their last reserves of food and were now reliant on what they could find if they were to not locate the

Bayaka by day's end. The cracking of new wood under the heat of the flames comforted Jenson as he approached the camp. The smell of the fire reminded him of home, where not long ago he awoke to a typical day before being transported into another world.

'Sleep well?' Jenson queried as he strolled into camp. He was hoping the fresh light of day would provide some perspective for the both of them after yesterday's conversation.

Kofi gave a subdued nod as he slowly packed his gear into the rucksack at his feet.

'Looks as though we're not far away from the ridge you spoke about,' Jenson continued.

'Just a few hours' hike downstream to get over the ridge,' Kofi finally muttered. 'From there they should be an hour or so further on.'

It wasn't the reception Jenson had hoped for but he was buoyed by the ground they had made to find themselves less than a day away from reaching the Bayaka. He was conscious of the state of affairs back at Headquarters and wanted to provide the data that could potentially find the solution to SK01. He was still coming to terms with the name of the disease.

Silent Killer? Who comes up with these anyway? He packed his bag and scurried after Kofi, feeling his joints pop and crack as his body warmed to the idea of hauling itself through another day. The bruises and scrapes he sustained from the hippo attack were beginning to become more troublesome as the constant humidity and moisture of the jungle prevented the wounds from drying out and healing. He still couldn't believe he'd walked away from the situation with just the flesh wounds he was troubled by. He finally caught up to Kofi as the jungle gave way to an open section of grassland that was at the foot of the ridge. Primate calls echoed through off the rock surface as they emerged from the densely forested undergrowth into the bright sunshine of the plain. The sun soaked Jenson's bones and for a moment he felt lighter than air. Maybe it was the lack of food or the stifling humidity of the Congo but he began to chuckle to himself. Here he was, sporting wounds from a hippo attack searching for a mysterious tribe in the Congo River Basin with a man he didn't know in search of answers for a disease crippling the populated world.

'Why are you laughing?' Kofi turned and asked.

'You know what, I have no idea!' Jenson replied as Kofi started to laugh from Jenson's infectious cackle.

Before long the two could no longer walk in a straight line and had to stop to catch their breath between bursts of hysterics. They were almost as loud as the chimpanzees who seemed to join in their outburst.

'You know what?' Kofi finally was able to say as their laughter slowly subdued. 'I am very glad to have met you, Dr Jenson Ryder.'

'Likewise.'

The pair pushed on, occasionally bantering each other with the contagious song of their laughter. As they approached the ridge, the terrain grew increasingly treacherous. Loose ground frequently slipped under their feet, creating rock falls. The distant echo of fallen earth below them was a constant reminder that one mistake could cost them their lives. Soon they were climbing a near-vertical face, clinging to whatever they could find to leverage their weary bodies ever higher. The straps of their rucksacks drove deep into their shoulders and the rising sun burned Jenson's exposed skin. Sweat cascaded down his face as he grimaced to haul himself onto a ledge. He looked down to see Kofi below him, striving for the same ledge to get some respite. At that moment, the sapling he entrusted his life with gave way, its shallow roots too weak to support the weight of a grown man.

'Kofi!' Jenson screamed as he saw him slide down the ridge face, desperately clawing to anything that he could.

The momentum at which he fell was too rapid to stop. Jenson pleaded for something, anything, to stop Kofi from sliding further and further down the cliff face. Peering over the edge, Jenson met Kofi's widening eyes. He could see the fear inside him as he stood hopelessly above in relative safety. A deafening silence then ensued as he lost sight of his friend. He was left with nothing but the sound of the wind in his ears and the distant crash of rocks hitting the ground far below.

'Kofi!' Jenson yelled. 'Kofi!' The desperation in his voice grew.

Once again, he was left with nothing but the air he breathed and the whistle of the wind as company. Climbing down the steep rocky face, fearing the worst, he had no idea what to do if he found Kofi motionless at the bottom. Reaching an overhang in the descent, he peered over the ledge to locate any signs below. Instead, he saw Kofi right in front of him, clinging to his life by the tips of his fingers, his legs dangling in mid-air.

'Grab my hand!' Jenson yelled as he lay down on his stomach, reaching over to assist. Kofi's desperation deepened as his grip on the rocky ledge grew weaker and more precarious by the second.

'I can't reach, Jenson. If I take one hand off, I'm gone!'

'If you don't grab my hand you're gone anyway. You've got to try. Let go of the pack,' Jenson pleaded. It's only weighing you down.'

'You know I can't do that. It has everything in it that is keeping us and this mission alive.'

He was right, Jenson knew it as well as Kofi. All the data-gathering instruments were in that pack, plus their remaining food, albeit scarce.

For what seemed an eternity, Kofi clung to life one minuscule slip at a time. The sweat from his hands loosened his grip further.

'Kofi, you *have* to try to grab my hand. Once I have you in my grip, I'll pull you up. I promise.'

Moments passed. The painstaking decision reverberating through Kofi's mind reflected the expression on his face. His cheeks grimaced, eyes darting, desperate and scared. Then a hand slipped a centimetre too far, leaving him with seconds to spare under an ever-weakening single-handed grasp. Without thought, Jenson lunged forward as best he could from the awkward position he found himself in and latched hold of Kofi's arm. Every muscle in his body strained as he inched him up, dragging his body over the ledge to safety. Both of them were drenched in sweat and panting from exhaustion, their chests heaving to reel the oxygen into their lungs.

'You're a stubborn bastard,' Jenson finally managed to say between breaths. 'You weren't going to let that pack go, were you?'

Kofi smiled and shook his head, still shaking from the adrenaline pulsating through his veins. 'I learn from the best.'

After taking some time to compose themselves and digest the gravity of what had just occurred, the pair dusted themselves off and began climbing once again, this time with a little more caution to each step. Eventually, they reached the top of the ridge without further mishap and were rewarded with a spectacular view of the vast stretches of forest around them. Their eyes followed the Congo River as it snaked through the trees and out into open grasslands all the way to the horizon. The vast, densely packed jungle cradled the water as it meandered to its next destination. Bursts of sunshine cut through breaks in the clouds, illuminating the brilliance of the tree canopy and the deep hue of the water. The wild beauty of the place was truly breathtaking in Jenson's eyes.

'You know, I think I'd take the events of the past few days again to get a view like this,' he said in a soft tone as he continued to scan the horizon.

'You're saying you would risk my life for a view?' Kofi protested in jest.

Jenson replied with a smile, still awe-struck by his surroundings.

Catching their breath with a break and soaking in the achievement of scaling a ledge that almost took a life, Jenson and Kofi began what they hoped would be their final stretch to meet the Bayaka tribe. The sun was beginning to get lower in the sky and Jenson was desperate to find them before the day was out. The large rocky outcrop they found themselves on soon descended into the web of vines and shrubbery once again, slowing their speed of travel to an agonising halt. Jenson's mind began to wander to his task at hand as he anticipated meeting the tribe. He would need to collect the data as soon as possible and ship it back to Abel along with GPS coordinates for their extraction. He had become so immersed in the ways of the jungle that he had largely forgotten about the trials of the outside world. He knew there would be an element of sadness to leave this place, even if he was sick to death of requiring a machete to clear any walkable path.

'Can you smell that?' Kofi turned to Jenson with a wide-eyed expression.

Jenson stopped but could not catch wind of anything. 'Campfire smoke. We are close!'

The excitement was clear in Kofi's voice. Despite their earlier conversation and conflict, Jenson was glad to see he still had the same emotional attachment to his people as he expected. It was human nature to want to be accepted, to be a part of something larger than just your own thoughts and routines. A few minutes later, Jenson smelt the familiar aroma of a campfire and began to walk that little bit faster in anticipation. It was then he felt the strange twinge and pain of something in the side of his neck. Thinking it was nothing more than the Jurassic mosquitos in this part of the world, he reached up to slap it away. Instead, he found a dart protruding from his neck and was suddenly overcome by a growing haze of white before he lost consciousness altogether. He staggered a few metres before he fell to the ground with a solid thud.

The blurry outlines of Kofi's face hovered above him as Jenson came to. He had no idea how much time had passed and little recollection of how he had become unconscious. Gingerly, he looked around to see he was lying on a stretcher bed within a small hut. The scent of earth and grass hung heavy in the room as he gradually sat up and tried to gather his bearings. The faint sound of voices could be heard from outside the walls, their words indecipherable in competition with the ringing in his ears. The hut was small, no more than three square metres and had a solitary open-air window, which allowed a stream of light to cast in on the floor. Jenson spread the hanging vines that acted as a doorway and feebly stepped out into the open. Several people milled around the other huts that surrounded the one he was in and a large fire acted as the centrepiece around the constructions.

We're here, Jenson said softly to himself as he slowly walked further out into the open. *The Bayaka.*

'Jenson. Jenson!' It was Kofi. 'You're awake. How are you feeling? I'm so sorry, my people do not take strangers lightly in this part of the jungle.'

'What happened?' Jenson's face was still a shade of grey even under the fading light and glow of the campfire.

'We were approaching the camp when we were spotted by Bayaka scouts. They did not recognise you so sedated you with a dart,' Kofi replied in a matter-of-fact tone.

'A dart? Just because they didn't know who I was?' His mind was incredibly foggy, so he didn't have the strength or concentration to argue that he thought that was a ridiculous reason to knock someone unconscious. Besides, he had finally made it to his destination to conduct the much-needed research that had the potential to save millions. The details of the past few hours could wait; what couldn't was to be introduced to the tribe and have them accept him. Luckily, Kofi was channelling a similar line of thinking as he gently ushered him by the arm towards the congregation of people around the fire.

'They will like you,' he whispered to him as they staggered over.

The introductions went smoothly and before long Jenson was welcomed with traditional custom and festivities. His head was still spinning as people danced into the night around the fire and plates of food were passed around at will. Kofi's smile seemed to return as he mingled with his tribe. A tinge of sadness hit Jenson's heart as he remembered their conversation.

What happened? Jenson wondered once more.

CHAPTER 21

Morning light brought fresh hope and a sense of purpose. Jenson's head was clear, as was his mission to obtain the vital data his team at Headquarters so desperately sought. He thanked powers beyond his control that the majority of their equipment remained intact despite being set upon by a raging hippo and on the verge of falling from a cliff.

In a matter of moments, the gear was prepared and ready for data collection. Kofi was once again by his side ready to assist. This was really the simple part though. Technological advancements from the military and health sectors had combined to create tools that provided data you could only dream about a decade ago. It was almost a matter of simply 'point and shoot'. Thermal imaging, cerebral fMRI and a range of neurological biomarkers could be collected without invasive procedures. It was almost scary what could be done without a subject knowing what was happening. Kofi looked on in a composite of admiration, confusion and fear, but remained silent throughout the hours Jenson worked. The raw data streamed in and simultaneously uploaded to a tiny data drive that would then be sent back to Abel in Lisala via drone. The fact that the data was there but practically indecipherable in its current form was almost a form of torture for Jenson. The answers lay in those numbers but he didn't have the code to unlock their meaning. For a moment he felt more like a mule than an ecologist, being the brute that gets the material and hands it over to more capable individuals. He recalled the last week and quickly renounced the thought and gave a smile to Kofi who remained peering over his shoulder, seemingly oblivious to the stream of data coming in and its potential.

The data capture allowed Jenson to interact with the Bayaka tribe and Kofi was more than willing to introduce him to those around camp at the time. He had the privilege of talking extensively with the leader of this tribe and was able to delve further into their way of life and outlook on the world.

'We call ourselves Bisi Ndima, which means people of the forest. We have been people of the forest for generations but now it is becoming harder and harder with the land getting smaller and smaller. We cannot go into National Parks to hunt and logging has caused our territory to become inhabitable.'

Jenson listened intently as the tribal Chief spoke of past generations' stories of slavery and exploitation. Amid the horror of their past emerged a spark of solidarity and with it a happiness. The type of happiness that arises from the simplicity of day-to-day life.

'We are still Bisi Ndima. The forest provides everything we need to live a good life. So long as the forest is here, we will be too.'

'How much information do you receive from what is happening outside in the rest of the world?' Jenson spoke inquisitively.

'We get reports of major events from time to time, mainly from Kofi. Apart from that, we keep to ourselves. The way of the forest has supported us and we will continue to live off our lands. Our people are happy to live that way. We have no need or desire for the outside world's contributions to our way of life. Look around you – we are happy and peaceful.' The Chief's eyes were jet black with his surrounding face crevassed with the years of his life. Spindly, curly grey hair poked out from his head and eyebrows and his cheekbones protruded high upon his face.

Jenson was intrigued by this man. His wisdom was unquestionable and he possessed a ruthlessness that was blanketed by kindness and sound reason that he had not encountered in anyone else.

'Can I ask you something else?' Jenson said gently.

The Chief could predict the next sentence that was going to come from his mouth and gave a smile that softened his face as he nodded. 'Kofi.'

Jenson paused and looked towards the ground as he thought about his next words. 'What happened? Why was he exiled from the tribe?'

There was a long silence as the Chief contemplated what to say.

'That is not a matter for anyone else but the Bayaka. Kofi knows what he has done and what he needs to do to reclaim the trust of his people.'

Jenson nodded in recognition of the statement but couldn't help but express his disappointment at the answer. After spending a week with Kofi and experiencing the highs and lows of the expedition, he had come to think of him as more than just his guide; he was almost a brother to him now.

'It is not for you to understand, young man,' the Chief continued. 'Part of what makes us who we are as a people is the fact that we are not fully understood by others. We are our own people and we live in our own way. We do not need the noise from outside to come into our lives.'

Jenson nodded again. 'I understand, trust me. There is too much going on outside of this forest that is contributing to the decline in our world.'

'That is why you are here? To understand what makes the Bayaka special and bring that back to others?' It was more of a statement than a question. He knew there was something else behind Jenson's presence in the tribe than pure intrigue. Nobody came this far into the Congo Basin without an ulterior motive.

The two of them sat quietly next to the cooking fire as the sun set on another day, both reflecting on their conversation. The serenity of their village was so beautiful it almost brought a tear to Jenson's eyes. To see people so happy and living so simply was something he hadn't witnessed for a long time. His mind flashed back to the few days he and Abel spent in Tokyo. There was nothing more haunting than the café they visited on the final day. The soul of everyone in that building had been destroyed by the very concrete they had paved to make life 'easier'.

Every single person's face was illuminated by the harsh white glare of a screen, their shoulders hunched, their eyes fixated and lifeless. The scene before him now portrayed the polar opposite. The scent of wood smoke drifted through the village among calls of laughter and children playing. The trees at this time of the evening created a spectrum of green that could create its own rainbow and the birdsong was more beautiful than any piece of music that could be created by mankind. There was no concrete. There was no electricity, no WiFi, no television or social media to distract them. Jenson was reminded of the adage that there is beauty in simplicity. In that very moment, there was nothing more resounding than that statement. He took a sip of the tea he had been given and smiled as he looked over at the Chief who was stoking the fire ready for the evening meal.

By nightfall, the data collection was complete and Jenson began the process of interpreting some of the raw numbers that were coming through. His primary objective was to get a copy of it to Abel as soon as possible, so he set up the compact drone they had 'carefully' transported all this way and uploaded the files to its body. Along with the data, he coded a message to Abel with the details of his extraction, including the required time and GPS coordinates. Kofi had indicated there was an area of flat ground approximately fifteen kilometres away from the village where a helicopter could land. Before being air-lifted out, Jenson had the integral task of continuing to monitor the tribe in the hope of understanding them on a deeper level – something the data could not provide. As an ecologist, this was his area of expertise and his field notes would complement the findings from the data already collected. His earlier reflections on the trip to Tokyo when compared to this sparked a thought in him that hadn't occurred before today. The current approach of tackling SK01 was clearly not working, so he decided to take a different tack and note the sociological aspects of Bayaka life that he deemed significant.

CHAPTER 22

Abel paced around the room of the hotel, ever anxious to hear word from Jenson. He was several days overdue in reporting to base and there were not only concerns for his safety but the integrity of CINS and their SK01 mission. He would have to report back to Hiram in the morning and at this stage, there was nothing new he could tell him. Jenson was still AWOL and they were no closer to getting the data they required. A gentle breeze fluttered the thin white curtains allowing the last of the day's light to creep in. The heat of Lisala was beginning to get to him. The humidity became oppressive through the middle of the day and as the sun broke through the storm clouds it became an oppressive soup of moisture and heat broiling the earth beneath it. The stench of the surrounding city sauntered among the waves of heat and only added to Abel's displeasure of the place. He was about to take a cold shower before the day was out to help him sleep. It was then he heard the distinctive high-pitched hum of a drone at his hotel window. Almost simultaneously, the alarm on his phone began to ring, informing him of its presence. He swiped the phone open and began the delicate task of landing the copter in the middle of his room.

'At last,' Abel said under his breath as the rotors slowed to a halt. He pulled the drive out from the underside of the device and began uploading the data to his laptop. Within minutes, it was sent to Headquarters with an update on Jenson's status. He was to be extracted in two days from the coordinates provided. The question now was what to do next. Abel supposed it was now dependent on the interpretation of the data and additional findings from Jenson's work in the field. With some structure and a rough plan, he was finally able to relax a little and take some time to rest his weary eyes. Stepping into the shower, he let a stream of cool water run down his face, neck and back, softening his muscles in the process. He stood there for what seemed like hours, propping himself against the cold tiled wall and tried not to think about SK01, even if it was for a moment.

Across vast expanses of ocean on the other side of the world, Hiram sat upright in his office chair. It was late into the night and only a skeleton of lighting illuminated the offices of Headquarters. He too was growing impatient with the lack of progress and if he was being honest, there was a streak of fear creeping in as well. He rubbed his narrow eyes, scraping his hands down the stubble of his unshaven cheeks and pondered what more could be done. In that moment he was alerted to the email notification in the bottom corner of his screen and saw the preview. He immediately clicked it to open the email and saw the files containing the data they had been so patiently waiting for. He hoped the answers to solving the plague of SK01 could be extracted from this array of numbers. He had Nya on the phone in an instant to get her and Emerson to work on deciphering it all. This was something that couldn't wait.

Nya came into Hiram's office shortly after, her eyes shadowed with fatigue after being woken from his phone call. Despite the hour of the night, she remained composed and spoke in her usual manner, almost excited to retrieve the information that lay hidden in the data she was about to delve into. Her dark brown hair hung loosely across her shoulders, with her fringe draping over the corners of her glasses. Emerson worked alongside her as they pulled the first sets of data and began what was to be a long night of arduous work.

Hours passed as the pair of them tirelessly worked in the dimly lit offices. Eventually, the first glimpses of natural light peered through the windows, bringing context to the time of day and their surroundings.

No miraculous breakthroughs had occurred in the hours of darkness, deflating Hiram's morale when he came to check on their progress.

'There doesn't seem to be any signs that a virus or vector has penetrated those who are presenting signs of illness. This is despite the neurological scans depicting otherwise.' Nya instructed Hiram. 'What I find most intriguing is that there are no physiological signs of a foreign body in the sick patients with the current data we have.' She pointed to the various scans and indicators on the screens before them. 'But as you can see from the fMRI real-time data is that there is a clear distinction in the synaptic activity between healthy and sick individuals.' Coloured diagrams of the brains of subjects flicked up on the screen to portray her point.

'So what you're saying is that there are signs of illness but they are not representative of a true virus or communicable disease?' Hiram responded.

'Correct.' Emerson chimed in. 'So we either have an entirely new class of infectious agent on our hands that we cannot detect or we're still looking in the wrong place.'

Hiram buried his head into the palms of his hands and took a deep breath. Half of the world's population, which included those who would be researching to find an answer, would soon be overrun with the very thing they were trying to stop. He knew it was only a matter of time before his own team were at risk as well.

'Suggestions then?' Hiram said, as he continued to scan through the collage of data on the screens in front of him.

'It's simple,' Nya replied quickly. 'We need more data from the field. But not just hard data from neurological tissue and scans. We need observational reports.' She looked over to Emerson for backup. He simply shrugged and nodded.

'The last update from Abel had Jenson's extraction in a little under thirty-six hours. We'll have his field notes and thoughts following that. But you're suggesting we need more than that?'

'I'm saying we need data to back up what we have here.' She spread her arms around the expanses of the room. 'At the moment, we have a sample of N equals two. We have those in Tokyo who are violently ill across the board and we have those who are seemingly unaffected in a remote pocket of the Congo. We need Jenson to confirm his sightings in the Congo are not an isolated case. We already know that Tokyo isn't but surely there's an explanation behind the anomalies that are dotted across the globe.'

Hiram nodded in agreeance and seemed surprised as to the sheer level of sense Nya made after not sleeping for a day. Her composure astounded him, which was the highest of compliments coming from the man who was imperturbable beyond any level in most circumstances.

'Right, can you collate a list of populations or locations that will provide additional data to complement the recent capture from the Congo?' Hiram swivelled on the glassy white tiles to return to his office when Nya immediately replied.

'Here you go, sir.' She handed him a single sheet of paper with a handful of destinations. 'There are very few locations that contain consistent reports of no SK01 presence as we identified in the Congo.'

Hiram looked at the list and cringed at the places that she had compiled. Quite simply, they were brutally inhospitable.

'It's my opinion that if we're to back up these findings, we need to gather data from the indigenous populations of Eastern Siberia, Greenland or Alaska.'

'Very well,' Hiram replied bluntly. 'I'll contact Abel and begin organising Jenson's next movements. I have contacts in Greenland that should allow us to enter the country on short notice.'

Within the space of a few phone calls, the fate of Jenson's next expedition had been decided. Hiram had contacted the Danish authorities and negotiated his arrival in Greenland and permission to undertake scientific research. It was then a matter of informing Abel and letting him take care of the finer details such as transport and resources.

Jenson was to investigate the Tunumiit people of Greenland, an Inuit population on the eastern part of the island. Like the Bayaka, they remained largely isolated from the influences of the outside world and continue to live in a traditional way: hunting seals, whales and other marine animals using dog mushing and kayaks as their transportation. There would be little rest between boarding a flight in the Congo's capital, Kinshasa, to landing in Nuuk, the capital of Greenland. He would then need transportation to the isolated town of Daneborg on the eastern seaboard. Hiram and Abel discussed logistics and the timeframe required for data retrieval. Appropriate clothing, supplies and equipment would be provided upon their arrival into Nuuk, along with details for Jenson's scientific goals. Hiram placed the phone carefully back on the receiver and leaned back in his chair. He looked out to Nya and Emerson, deep in discussion. Without hearing a word of their conversation, he could almost sense the back and forth as they deliberated the data before them. Jenson's findings had presented more questions than answers but Hiram sensed a renewed optimism despite this. At least they had direction and could eliminate some avenues that they had been previously pursuing. As long as he had hope, he felt they would find an answer to SK01.

CHAPTER 23

Abel boarded the helicopter as the engine slowly ramped into full swing. By the time he was buckled into his seat beside the pilot with his headset on, the blades were roaring loudly above his head. The relatively peaceful surroundings were transformed into the intermittent belting of the blades slicing the air. It had seemed an eternity since Abel had last seen Jenson and he privately admitted he almost missed his presence. He had grown fond of Dr Ryder since he joined the team and saw the deep level of commitment he had towards the pursuit of finding an answer to SK01.

Soaring high above the jungle canopy provided an immense perspective to the task that Jenson and Kofi had completed by navigating these lands to find the Bayaka. Abel looked over the horizon in awe as the helicopter flew with ease, honing in on the GPS coordinates provided by Jenson. After a few hours and several conversations in broken English over the radio communications with the pilot, Abel finally spotted the landing site. Jenson had laid out signals to confirm their location and before long he was face to face with his new colleague once again.

'What took you so long?' Jenson said with a smile, as Abel hopped out of the cockpit.

'It's good to see you too, Dr Ryder,' Abel replied, shaking his hand.

Kofi lingered in the background. Like a son who was about to say goodbye to his father, it was hard to tell if he was sad or excited. They loaded the supplies into the rear of the helicopter and in an instant, Abel's suit and tie were covered in dust and sweat, although he didn't seem fazed. The early morning sun crested over the hilltop to the east, which prompted the outburst of primate calls from the shadows of the jungle around them. Small birds fluttered beneath the cooling engine of the helicopter in pursuit of insects that hummed above the thick green grass.

Jenson turned towards Kofi with a look of resignation and opened his arms.

'I guess this is us,' he said, not knowing how else to say goodbye. 'I can't thank you enough for everything you've done. You're not just a friend but a brother. We will see each other again someday. Of that, I am sure.'

Kofi hugged Jenson exuberantly, slapping his back so as not to squeeze him too hard. 'Thank you, Jenson.'

It was all he managed to say before Jenson boarded the aircraft with Abel and the engine drowned out any chance of conversation. As they rose higher into the air, the knot in the back of Jenson's throat grew larger. It was the unexpected friendship that made his relationship with Kofi so special and so difficult to walk away from. He had come to the Congo with a single task in mind but was now leaving with so much more.

It wasn't until Abel gestured for Jenson to put on his headset after half an hour into the flight that he started to debrief him on the standing of the mission. Abel explained the orders passed down from Hiram on what Jenson's next expedition would involve. It came as a shock to him, as he thought they would be heading back to HQ after leaving Lisala. Evidently, this was not to be the case and a renewed enthusiasm was fostered inside of him, quelling the grief of saying goodbye to Kofi ever so slightly.

'We're going to Greenland?' Jenson replied over the crackling headset.

Abel nodded before replying. 'Correct, we need to replicate the findings of the data you collected here before we can have any confidence in making a decision around them.' There was silence for a moment while Jenson digested the details.

'Abel,' he finally said. 'It's bloody cold in Greenland and I don't have any warm clothes.'

He smiled, missing the clever wit that Jenson displayed on a regular basis. 'You should know me better than that by now, Dr Ryder. Don't worry, the details have all been taken care of.'

The helicopter touched down in Kinshasa. The heat from the tarmac was oppressive as they stepped from the cockpit. As he levered himself down from the helicopter, Jenson began to wonder how he would adapt to the climate in Greenland in less than twenty-four hours' time. He was also slightly shell-shocked with the sudden onslaught of noise, pollution and human contact. It was strange for him to be surrounded by foreign noises, sounds and concrete for as far as the eye could see. This, along with the absence of green, the heat and humidity caused a wave of nauseousness to sweep over him.

'This way, Dr Ryder,' Abel interrupted. 'We have the plane ready for take-off.'

Jenson's eyes were directed towards a private jet that lay in isolation on a small patch of the runway. A few ground staff mingled at its wheels, shimmering in the heat waves reflecting from their feet. Jenson picked up his bag and walked towards the plane. Its sleek and slender lines reflected the afternoon sun in a haze of jet fumes.

Climbing aboard the stairs and into the main entrance, Jenson was greeted with a blast of air-conditioned cool air that sucked the sweat from his skin. A bar embossed the main area with a few cream leather seats and lounges around it. The luxuriousness of it all caused a sense of guilt to deepen in his stomach. He'd been sleeping on hessian sacks and goat hides for the past week.

'I'll take your bags for you, sir, and we'll be up in the air in no time,' a concierge said as she strolled through the cabin. 'Please, take a seat and make yourself at home. Would you like a drink? Perhaps a champagne?'

'Ah, sure.' Jenson hesitated. 'Thank you.'

He sat in the soft leather chair and briefly reflected on the accomplishment of his first mission. The champagne, he levelled with himself, would help that process.

CHAPTER 24

Sirens and chaos dominated the streetscape as emergency services worked in overdrive to accommodate the sick. Sasha waited patiently as the ambulance took Michelle away in a vegetative state, her spirits barely altered even with the addition of fluids through an intravenous drip. The look in her eyes said everything. She seemed resigned to her fate of being incapable and obsolete. In all her time on this earth, Sasha had never seen a look so haunting peer out of the eyes of another human being. It wasn't until she took another shower the following morning that the very same look emanated from her own face. Her gaunt, ghostly figure stared back at her in resignation through the fog of the mirror. Her usually radiant blonde hair looked dull and thin, ageing her well beyond her years. Her clothing was dishevelled no matter what she wore or how long she took to correct it.

Outside, more cries for help echoed down the street. Harrowing wails had been coming over the back fence all night. Another casualty of what was now referred to as SK01. News outlets ran nothing else on their stations but updates on the ill and the latest developments. Inevitably, false words had spread just like the SK01 plague itself. Some reports were indicating that half the world's population had been decimated in the past few months alone. Human extinction was a very real threat, one station had reported. It was hard to decipher what to believe amidst the panic and mayhem of daily life. Sasha had stopped calling work to say she wasn't coming in for the day. She'd been in once since the arrival of SK01 but when she arrived, the office space was abandoned.

Not a soul was around to answer her calls as she drifted through the empty office chairs and blank computer screens. Fluorescent lights hummed above her head, mimicking the static in her brain as she took in the scene of abandonment before her. She sat down on a lonely office chair, feeling the weight of her body compress into the cushioning. She stared through bleary eyes at the photos of loved ones at a stranger's desk.

Would they still be alive? She shocked herself with how emotionless and heartless the thought arose. It was like she had been hollowed from the inside out and was now walking around with mere bones and flesh. A single-celled organism in a human body.

Walking the empty streets on her way home, she spied people peering through the curtains of their houses and apartments as the unfamiliar sound of footsteps passed their front door. Their faces mirrored her depletion and anxiety about what was to come. It seemed the emotion of fear was the only thing people had in common now.

Entering her house, she was almost suffocated by the stench of sweat and lack of fresh air. The fridge hummed noisily in the kitchen as it worked through the rising temperature. The TV rattled in the background with incessant reports of illness and panic on the streets of major cities throughout the world. Looting had started to become an issue as a number of shop owners were forced to abandon their businesses due to ill health. Sasha checked her phone that sat on the bench beside the kitchen sink. Still no word from Jenson, or from anyone for that matter. A feeling of isolation crept over her as she thought of the prospect of her own death. She never pictured it being like this. Alone and confused at the mercy of a worldwide plague. Nobody could prepare themselves for that, she thought. It was then she heard the familiar words from the news presenter on her TV.

CINS Chief Operating Officer Hiram Nebu has been identified as the man leading the fight against SK01. He has compiled a team of specialists in the field with reports that local academic Dr Jenson Ryder is a contributor to.

Sasha's mind trailed off as the reporter continued to speak but she was lost.

'Jenson?' she said softly under a tired breath.

That was why he wasn't responding to her phone calls or text messages. He was the one trying to stop all this! Tears trickled from her eyes as she thought of him and a small sob leaked from her throat as she sat on the couch by the television. She wasn't sure if it was relief, fear or hope that she was feeling. Her aching mind had become too tired to decipher even her own emotions. She did seek solace in the fact that if there was anyone in the world who could solve such an insurmountable obstacle, it was Jenson.

CHAPTER 25

Jenson made his way across the frozen tarmac into the airport. The warmth of the jet was hard to let go of and the shock of arriving into Greenland had well and truly set in. His shivering body nestled in the back of a golf cart as it painstakingly crept towards the warmth of nearby buildings. The driver spoke little English and simply laughed when Jenson hopped on.

'Not warm! Cold!' he had said with a broad, enthusiastic smile written across his face.

While Jenson had the opportunity to take a shower on the plane, his clothing for the next expedition was to be collected in Nuuk. He looked quite the sight as he was whisked away from a private jet in shorts and a t-shirt in the middle of a Scandinavian winter. The cold bit at his flesh, his teeth chattered and his body convulsed into a fit of shiver as he tried hopelessly to get warm again. Ice formed around his nose and eyes and a coat of white snow dusted his unshaven cheeks. If this was to be an omen for the upcoming task, he didn't like it all. Abel provided little sympathy as he too looked hypothermic in his suit and tie. He somehow didn't let down his unflappable guard and proceeded to direct Jenson with his usual prose.

'This way, Dr Ryder.' He indicated towards a long hallway that would lead them to their ground transportation.

Abel parked the car near an obscure-looking building on the outskirts of Nuuk and braced himself before pulling the door latch to enter the freezing temperature outside. Jenson was instructed to stay put while Abel collected their supplies. There was no argument from his perspective, with the outside temperature well below zero. Not long after, Abel returned with two burly Greenlandic men who shouldered the bulk of the gear. The car bounced and shook as they heaved everything in the boot. All Jenson could think about was getting changed into thermals and a down jacket.

'We're not far from the hotel. You can get into your gear once we arrive there,' Abel instructed.

'Aye-aye, Captain,' he replied in a monotone voice.

After a hot shower, which lasted well over half an hour, and dressing himself in copious amounts of clothing, Jenson finally stopped shivering and felt a wave of lethargy overcome him. He sat in a high-backed leather chair in front of a laptop where he began his debrief over video conference with Hiram and the team at Headquarters. The constant effort to stay warm had sapped his energy and as he sat there in the warm hotel room, his eyes and mind began to drift. He struggled to concentrate on the specifics of what Nya, Emerson and Hiram were talking about. It was as though he was back at school acting as the student who was about to drift off to sleep and fall face first into his textbook.

There was a knock at the hotel door and shortly after, a man dressed in black and white attire came in with room service, which included a thick black coffee. If there was one luxury he missed while out in the Congo Basin, it was his morning brew. The perfect antidote to Jenson's hypothermic-induced semi-coma; the bitter, tar-like liquid coated his throat and immediately, he became alert again. He could feel the warmth of the liquid reach his stomach and radiate from the inside out. The caffeine was simultaneously pulsing through his bloodstream, dilating his vascular system and exciting the neurons in his central and peripheral nervous system. Suddenly, he felt whole again.

The others continued to talk as unbeknownst to them, Jenson was slowly coming back to life. They had been speaking about the discrepancies between the neural imaging data between sick and healthy individuals. There was clearly something structural occurring in the central nervous system but it couldn't be explained by a virus or bacteria based on the data that had been collected so far. Nya expressed her frustration at seeing a clear pathology at play with no semblance of a vector to attribute it to.

'What if we've got it all wrong?' Jenson suddenly interrupted, catching them all off-guard as he had been completely silent for the past ten minutes. 'What if we're looking at this from the wrong angle?'

There was a large pause as the others contemplated his statement.

'You may need to elaborate, Jenson.' Hiram finally spoke.

'I think we've been looking at this pathology from the wrong perspective. You've just said it has no vector; it's not viral, it's not bacterial, it's not contagious based on the way it's spreading. What if the body itself is the cause?' The steam from his mug swirled in front of the camera, disappearing into space. He took a sip and began to elaborate. 'What I'm proposing is that this is not a physical illness but a psychological one that is transposing itself into physical symptoms. I know you have probably heard of such things before but bear with me. What's the one thing all the large-scale healthy populations we know of have in common?'

There was silence on the other end of the line.

'They're geographically isolated.' Nya spoke with hesitation.

'Yes, but let's assume this isn't communicable.' More silence ensued. 'They're primitive. They're living a simpler life to those we see in places where SK01 is endemic.'

Jenson continued to talk for over an hour about his sudden insights into SK01. It was as though the coffee had infused him with the answers that were lying dormant inside of him all this time. Or perhaps the hypothermic rebound had catalysed a thought that was seated deep in his mind all along. All it needed to germinate was the frozen Greenlandic air followed up with a scolding hot shower and coffee as a chaser. Hiram, Emerson and Nya sat in silence as he spoke. They took notes on various points or checked their screens intermittently for the data that could provide backup to his hypotheses. What he proposed to them was relatively simple. The underlying cause of SK01 was the result of modern life and its associated impact on the psychological state. Constant exposure to artificial light, noise, noxious gases and other unknown pollutants had accumulated over a period of time and it was now reaching breaking point. Jenson suggested that perhaps everyone was affected, but only once a certain threshold is reached do people display the symptoms of the disease; the tangible signs that were now causing panic across the globe and sending humanity into the grips of chaos.

'Essentially the mind is in a protective state, retreating deep inside the body to preserve the necessary functions for survival for as long as possible; just like blood retreats to the central organs when we're cold, the nervous system is going into safe mode. We're dealing with a nervous system in a state of severe repression and angst.'

'These are bold claims, Jenson,' Hiram said after digesting the onslaught of information. 'We need solid evidence to back them up. Not until we have that can we begin a process of treatment. You must remember we're dealing with the entirety of the world's population here, not a small subset. Any interventions will have massive ramifications.'

His words hung in the air for a while. Deep down, this proposal was all they had. They needed a breakthrough and this was the best chance they had.

Jenson's plan was to travel to the community Nya and Emerson had identified on the Eastern seaboard of Greenland and obtain the same data collected while in the Congo. Combined with his field notes and observations, he hoped this would provide a correlation that supported the idea that contact with modern technologies and anthropomorphic intrusions were the reason behind the inoculation of SK01. While he knew this approach was going out on a limb, there was still a sense of self-assurance. Jenson had long been an advocate for a simpler life, his own living arrangement was a testament to that. The past two or three decades had brought monumental change to the way humans interacted with the world around them. There was now a disassociation with the natural elements and a shift to severely abnormal ways of living from an evolutionary perspective. Circadian rhythms and deep-seated biological needs were being altered, repressed or blatantly ignored. Such changes could not take place so rapidly without consequences. That was Jenson's hypothesis anyway.

The hesitation from the others was clearly evident as he continued to explain the nuances of his theory. Even across the other side of the world through the porthole of distant video communication, body language could still be perceived. Jenson could feel the weight of responsibility transfer to him as he now set about the task of supporting his claims with scientific evidence. He just hoped he wouldn't wake up tomorrow morning with some sort of hypothermic hangover and wonder what the hell he had been thinking.

Jenson said goodbye to his colleagues at Headquarters, delicately placed the lid of his laptop shut and took a deep breath. An eerie light was creeping through the windows of the hotel, a product of the sun just skimming the horizon for a few hours each day. Looking at the clock by his bedside, he found it hard to believe it was already after midnight. He would need some rest to tackle what was ahead of him. If Abel's initial briefing was anything to go by, there would be limited resources at his disposal for this data collection expedition. He needed every ounce of energy and mental strength he could muster and for that, he required sleep.

CHAPTER 26

Back at Headquarters, Hiram and the team discussed at length what Jenson had just proposed.

'It's certainly a hypothesis from left field,' Emerson stated to get the conversation running.

The new change in thought had been hard to acclimatise to and only added to their unease. It has been a strenuous few days with limited breakthroughs from the data obtained in the Congo and rising pressure from external parties who were desperate for something to reassure the world's ever-panicked population.

'My fear is not that Jenson is wrong but rather that he's correct.' Hiram paused as Nya and Emerson looked through his tired eyes, eager to hear why. 'Think about what we would need to do in order to quell the onset and progression of SK01 if his hypothesis is indeed true. The world would need to regress by decades, perhaps more. Restrictions to modern conveniences would need to be implemented, motorised transport would be reduced, everything that makes society tick in this day and age would become a target. It's a slippery slope and I'm not sure the world is ready for it.'

A stale silence hung in the air as they contemplated Hiram's forecast. He was right. If they found SK01 to be initiated from a psychological standpoint, the way humans lived would forever be altered in an effort to curb its widespread destruction.

'That's not something we have control over,' Nya finally replied. 'We have a duty of care to the rest of the world to find what is causing this. The damage it has done – the damage it is currently doing – is far worse than what you're proposing.'

Nya was right and Hiram knew it. He just couldn't bear to think of the inevitable conversation he would have with the UN and the WHO should this play out the way Jenson had described.

'At this stage, it is still a hypothesis. I need you two to identify whether it is true or not. That's the mission for now. We'll concern ourselves with the rest of it if and when it arises.'

Emerson and Nya nodded in agreeance and returned to their workstation and began the analysis process once more. Trawling through the mounds of data once again, they searched for any signs that could point to their new focus of attention.

Hiram's black shoes echoed on the white tiled floor as he slowly made his way back to his office. The journey seemed to become more and more lonely each time. His confidence and assurance in what they were pursuing was waning with each passing hour, and the strength and energy to portray otherwise was becoming exhausting. There was a limit to the amount of time he could tell himself that things would work out. It suddenly dawned on him that he could be succumbing to the illness himself. He wondered if Emerson and Nya could sense it too. Could they see through his façade and see the rising presence of a defeated man behind the curtain?

CHAPTER 27

Jenson woke to a howling wind, which was trying desperately to find a way through any gap in the hotel window. It screamed at him to get out of bed and start his next expedition but the fatigue from yesterday still lingered and he found the darkness of outside further consolidation to stay under the covers for slightly longer than usual. That was until Abel knocked at his door.

'Dr Ryder.' He still insisted on the formality. 'I'll debrief you on your expedition requirements in forty-five minutes.'

Jenson mumbled receipt of his request through the doorway and dragged his legs onto solid ground.

After another soaking hot shower, Jenson felt somewhat ready to tackle the day ahead. Abel began his overview of the next phase over a steaming bowl of porridge. Jenson savoured each warming mouthful, knowing that it may be his last warm meal out of the elements for a while. An array of maps and files were spread out over the table as they discussed their approach. The settlement in question was located just south of Daneborg, a small station on the eastern seaboard of the country which also served as the headquarters of Sirius Patrol, the world's most elite and extreme dog sled patrollers. Members of Sirius were aligned with the elite Danish Naval Unit and conducted long-range reconnaissance missions through the vast and barren stretches of ice that make up the Northeast Greenland National Park.

'This is the largest National Park in the world,' Abel said as he pointed to the area on the map in front of them. 'It's almost a million square kilometres in size, so you're going to need some local knowledge.'

Jenson's eyes swelled at the statistic and his heart skipped a beat; not in nervousness but rather anticipation. His lethargy and fatigue from transitioning to this icy, desolate country had suddenly been reversed with the thought of exploring the world's largest national park to search for a community that had operated the same way for hundreds, perhaps thousands of years.

'So who have you paired me up with this time?' Jenson asked.

Abel pulled a file from the stack next to his arm and handed it to Jenson. It contained the profile of a Sirius Patrol member, Aleksander Wolff. A man with twenty-five years of experience on the patrol as well as service in the SAS and Danish elite special forces. His picture portrayed a stereotypical Scandinavian man, with blonde short hair, glowing tanned skin and blue eyes. He had a weather-beaten appearance and masculine features, most prominent of which was his square jawline. His image reflected his impressive list of accomplishments out in the field. There was no questioning the credibility of this man in the cold desolate environment of Greenland. A sudden sense of inferiority hit Jenson as he leafed further through Wolff's file. He had turned from the outdoor specialist on the team to the scientist who needed protection from this strange and hostile white world and freezing temperatures. The level of training and expertise required to be a Sirius Patrol member was extreme. Rigorous camps in the frozen wilds of Greenland and the Faroe Islands over five weeks were just the beginning. In essence, the program was a case of last men standing. The final two candidates in the training course were selected for their first tour of Greenland, which consisted of twenty-six straight months of duty. Jenson tried to imagine the resilience and strength required to last over two years in the cold, dark expanses of this land. Flecks of ice spat against the window from another howling wind gust as he had the thought.

'The settlement you need to get to isn't in Daneborg itself, that's just the base for Sirius.' Abel continued. 'You'll be choppered in to meet

Wolff there and then use their sled dogs to reach the settlement. Spend as much time as you need collecting the data that's required. We need this to be steadfast, Dr Ryder.' Abel looked at Jenson with razor focus.

There was no questioning the stakes of this expedition. CINS was going all in on Jenson's theory and they needed solid proof before implementing the drastic changes that accompanied his hypothesis. A silence hung in the air as Abel let the gravity of the situation take hold. The air suddenly felt colder again with the realisation that the fate of his colleagues' reputation and the lives of millions rested in his hands. Jenson swivelled his spoon among the creamy bowl of hot oats and took a spoonful in consideration.

'Okay,' he finally said. 'So when do I leave?'

'Air transport arrives in four hours and you'll be in Daneborg by 1800 hours. From there, your schedule will be dictated by the weather and primarily by Wolff.'

Jenson looked down at the maps and files before him on the table and considered what he needed to do before setting off. There was limited information available on the customs and history of the settlement they would be travelling to after getting to Daneborg. So instead, he studied the geography of the region to understand the terrain they would be covering. He didn't want to arrive under-prepared and disgrace himself in front of one of the most decorated Sirius Patrol members to have ever served.

Abel had done everything possible to brief Jenson on the expedition. It was amazing what the man could do in such as short space of time and with limited sleep. He got up from the table and rolled the maps into neat piles and placed the files on Jenson's side table.

'That will be all from me,' he said as he stood up and buttoned his jacket. 'I wish you all the best out there, Dr Ryder; I really hope the answers can be found.'

With that, he turned and headed out the door, leaving Jenson grasping for a reply, only to see him walk out before he could muster anything worth saying. The door closed behind him, allowing a silence to enter the room that left Jenson wondering if he really should be the man for the job.

What on Earth am I doing? It was far too late to turn back now; the time for self-doubt had long passed. He thought back to the phone call with Hiram on the seemingly idle morning in this office. It seemed like an eternity, looking back now. If there was a time to quit, it would've been then.

To alleviate his growing nervousness, Jenson packed and re-packed his rucksack over and over again. He didn't want to leave anything vital behind but at the same time, he needed to be light and nimble on the trail to allow his data collection to be efficient and seamless. The conditions would be extremely adverse and extraneous items could be the difference between success and failure. It was a predicament he faced every time he prepared for a hike, bike-packing trip or field expedition; it was just the stakes were a little higher on this occasion. After what he thought was the sixth re-pack, he finally settled on the best equipment for the job and convinced himself that the gear he packed would keep him warm and dry; he desperately hoped it would. There was nothing left to do now but begin; the time for preparation was gone. With that thought, the distant sound of a helicopter made itself heard as it edged closer to Jenson's extraction point. The butterflies in his stomach fluttered that little bit harder.

CHAPTER 28

Jenson made his way to a nearby rooftop where the helicopter was due to touch down. At this point, he was more nervous about the rendezvous with Wolff than anything else. As he climbed the cold, dimly lit stairwell to the top, there was an immense sense of anticipation bubbling inside. He found it difficult to contain, almost sprinting up the final floor. With each flight of stairs, the crack of the rotor blades grew more prominent, serving to urge Jenson higher and higher. Bursting open the crude, small metal door out onto the roof, Jenson was hit with a wall of wind and ice that stung his face. The helicopter only made it worse as the rotors kicked up more and more fallen snow and recreated the sound of a hostile blizzard. Jenson ran with his head down and hunched over, trying to shield his face from the oncoming flecks of ice, all the while not wanting to be decapitated or lose a limb. His rucksack held snugly to his back as he trotted towards the passenger door and heaved it open. He shook the pilot's hand and then began to buckle himself in and fix his headset.

'Welcome,' a crackling voice said as Jenson fiddled with the controls on his ear.

'Ready to go?' the pilot asked.

Jenson have a thumbs up and then uttered 'let's go' into his comms system to give it a test. He gave a wry smile as the engine kicked into gear and the blades started to speed up.

Once in the air, the pilot introduced himself to Jenson. He was an ex-Sirius Patrol member himself and knew of Aleksander Wolff.

'His reputation is legendary in these parts.'

It appeared that nobody was more qualified or decorated in this part of the world than Wolff.

'Just don't piss him off, he might just leave you out there to freeze your arse off!'

A crackling laugh hollered down Jenson's headset as he looked over the grinning pilot. It was probably the last thing he wanted to hear at this stage as he was already on edge about meeting the man.

As they exited Nuuk, the landscape quickly turned from a frosted grey of concrete buildings to an expansive white that blanketed the entire surface below them. It was like another planet, especially after coming out of the Congolese jungle where the senses were overloaded with an array of sights, smells and sounds in every direction. Now there was nothing but a 360-degree view of a flat, icy, cold and hostile stretch of earth. They reached the coast on their way up to Daneborg, which provided some change in the scenery. Dramatic fjords jutted the coastline for hundreds of kilometres. They created a jigsaw of ice caps and nooks to which Jenson spotted seals, penguins and whales. It was hard to comprehend that any life at all could exist at these latitudes but the icy waters below were a nutrient-rich paradise and sanctuary for countless organisms both gigantic and minuscule. Jenson was transfixed as the helicopter seamlessly soared over the hostile land and heaving ocean below. The pilot seemed to pick up on Jenson's curiosity and awe and made a steady decline to get a closer look.

'Nowhere else quite like it, hey?' His voice crackled over the intercom.

Jenson looked over at him with a broad grin springing from his unshaven face. He felt like a kid being taken for a joyride.

'Incredible' was all he could reply with as they scouted the ice sheet. 'Simply incredible.'

Before long, a few buildings became visible in the distance – tiny red dots perched on the edge of a white abyss. If Jenson was to describe the village in a word, 'inhospitable' was what came to mind. There was an irrevocable bleakness that resonated from observing Daneborg in the air. The only thing that brightened its aesthetic was the red paint used on all the buildings. The pilot later informed him that it was purely to contrast with the white surroundings, so residents had a better chance of seeing the shacks in blizzards and whiteouts. There was also a historical reason for it. Red paint was traditionally cheap to produce as it was simply a matter of mixing ochre with cod liver oil.

'Plenty of that around here!' the pilot exclaimed as he brought the helicopter in to land nearby.

Jenson quickly removed his headset and jumped out with his rucksack slung over one shoulder. Eddies of snow and ice kicked up from the earth below as he staggered underneath the rotors to the relative calm and quiet of the village. He was assured that someone would be there to greet him. Before he knew it, the helicopter was a distant roar on the horizon and Jenson was left with nothing but the sound of the wind in his frozen ears and the sight of ice as far as the eye could see. Observing the village of Daneborg as he trudged towards it, a sense of nervous anticipation came over him; partly due to the hostile conditions and partly because he was eager to finally meet the most distinguished Sirius Patrol member to ever live.

A figure appeared from the main building as Jenson got closer. He was tall and decked head to toe in a snowsuit, large black boots and oversized mittens. His face was covered by the hood of his black suit and shielded with red goggles.

'Dr Ryder?' the man said as they finally reached each other on the icy stretch.

Jenson reached out to shake the man's hand. 'Please, call me Jenson. You must be Aleksander.'

He slapped him on the back with a heartiness that shocked his ribcage, taking Jenson off guard.

'Call me Wolff,' he replied over a gust of arctic wind. 'C'mon, let's get inside and brief you.'

A wave of warmth hit Jenson's body as they entered the red wooden shack that was to be his base for the foreseeable future. He brushed the snow and ice from his torso and dropped his bag by the door. A fire was burning in the pot-belly stove that nestled itself in the corner. Small windows on each side of the building let some natural light in; otherwise, it was illuminated by a solitary lightbulb dangling from the ceiling. Rustic shelves adorned the walls, which contained various items collected from years of sheltering Sirius. Tusks, horns, buoys and netting were just some of the items that decorated the room. Across from the stove was a small sink and tap perched on top of the bench with a metal bucket hanging from the pipes. Wolff showed him to his bunk, which resembled the bedrooms of a school camp. It might take some adjusting at first but Jenson was glad to finally be in Daneborg with Wolff to get the expedition underway.

'I'll let you settle in and then we can brief you on what the next few days will look like,' Wolff said as his boots echoed upon the wooden floorboards.

As he exited, all that was left was the sound of the wind relentlessly trying to creep through any gap in their little red structure. It would be Jenson's soundtrack for now and he was completely at ease with it.

That night, Jenson, Wolff and a fellow Sirius Patrol member, Astergaard, sat under a dim light bulb, eating reindeer stew as the wind continued to bellow. Astergaard, or 'Aster' as Wolff called him, was equally as intimidating as Wolff in his physical presence. Both had broad shoulders that were accentuated by the overalls and thick woollen jumper worn underneath. Aster seemed to be slightly younger than Wolff and certainly acted like his inferior when around him. Although his grasp of the English language was sound, he spoke infrequently and often nodded and observed as Wolff spoke about the expedition. After all, he would be the caretaker of Daneborg while he and Jenson were away. Wolff, on the other hand, spoke confidently and at times flippantly of what the process would be to get to the remote settlement south of Daneborg.

'We'll have a team of dogs with us, so it shouldn't take too long,' said Wolff as he slurped the juice and marrow out of a reindeer bone. 'Maybe two, three, four days at most. It depends on the weather, which is looking okay at the moment but it can change like *that*.' He clicked his fingers as he emphasised the last word.

Jenson was amazed at the size of Wolff's hands. They dwarfed the dinner plates they were using to eat off and his fingers were as thick and strong as iron rods from years of hard labour.

Jenson had several questions as Wolff talked him through the planning, but he refrained from interjecting at the risk of sounding dumb and also out of respect, something that seemed to radiate from his very presence. As he spoke, Wolff poured a clear liquid into three mugs and allocated them out to each man. Both Wolff and Aster took hearty sips to which Jenson dutifully followed only to choke as he swallowed what tasted like pure rocket fuel. He quickly jammed in a pile of stew to wash it down as the other men smiled at each other.

'You like it?' Wolff said, his steely blue eyes gazing out from under the glow of the light above.

Jenson smiled and nodded.

'Take it as the first step in your initiation. You'll grow to love it. It's the only thing that warms you up out here! And don't worry, there will be plenty more initiation steps for you to complete when you're in my company.' Wolff let out a hearty cackle and slapped Jenson on the shoulder, almost knocking him from his chair.

After dinner had been finished, including the juices being mopped up with stodgy homemade bread, Wolff got down to business. He unravelled a map of the area and splayed it across the table.

'We're here.' He pointed on the map. 'And we need to venture south through these fjord lands to reach the settlement. It's no cakewalk but I think we can get the job done efficiently.'

Suddenly the jovial attitude had completely dissipated from Wolff's demeanour and all that remained was a calculated and determined soldier prepping for a mission. His eyes changed from exuberant to a narrow focus that brought out an icy grey in his usual blue. This was no doubt part of the reason why he had been such as successful soldier and patrol member over a long and illustrious career. Jenson tried to mimic his teacher and guide by concentrating his focus on the maps before him.

The terrain looked ominous at best and a death trap at worst. They would venture down a coastline that was littered with sea ice and steep fjords that were constantly moving, making it treacherous to navigate. Jenson's knowledge of trekking in such landscapes was limited but he knew enough to realise that this was, as Wolff phrased it, 'no cakewalk'. As if to re-iterate his thoughts, a screaming blast of wind battered the shack, causing the lightbulb above them to rock methodically, shifting their shadows over the maps on the table.

After an hour of intense discussion with Wolff and Aster about their plans, they had come to a consensus that they would leave in seventy-two hours, leaving enough time for adequate preparation and for Jenson to acclimatise to both the conditions and the dogs he would be using as their transportation. It was the opportunity to try his hand at dog mushing that Jenson was most excited about. He had read stories of the famous Iditarod mushing race in Alaska and had a romantic notion of travelling across these vast stretches of frozen wilderness. In practice, however, it was far more skilful and taxing than he could ever have imagined. The rapport Wolff and Aster had with their team of dogs was mesmerising but it was clearly the product of years of training and experience in the field. On multiple occasions, Jenson got his lines tangled, fell off the sled and lost control of his lead dog. After some intense tuition and stern words from Wolff, he eventually got the basics covered, which would allow him to run his own team alongside Wolff down to the southern indigenous community. He was a long way off competing in the Iditarod, but he could at least tick something off his bucket list.

CHAPTER 29

A cold darkness greeted Jenson when he awoke. The windows were frosted over and reflected the light from his solitary bedroom lamp. He wiped the condensation away to peer into the outer world but was met with nothing but an eerie light from the stars casting their glow onto the ice. The wind seemed to have abated slightly, adding to the feeling of isolation and the sheer breadth of wilderness that lay on the other side of the wall. Today he would be venturing into that wilderness with nothing but the essentials for survival. As he dressed himself in layer upon layer of merino, goose down and Gore-Tex, he couldn't help but smile with excitement and anticipation. This could be the beginning of a moment that alters the course of humanity, while living out a boyhood fantasy at the same time.

He stoked the pot-belly stove to boil some water. Every ounce of warmth before beginning today now seemed critical, so he filled a vacuum flask with hot milky tea while sipping away at a mug at the same time. The warmth of the mug penetrated his hands, thawing them to the extent where he began to feel the sensations at the tips of his fingers again. The roughness of the wooden bench and silkiness of his jacket suddenly seemed more pronounced, as though his fingers were beginning to feel all over again.

Wolff knocked at his door and entered at the same time, his boots clobbering over the wooden floorboards.

'Ready?' he asked with a steely resolve.

Jenson nodded in reply and followed him outside after finishing the rest of his steaming mug of tea. Wolff had the dogs ready to go; their cacophony of excited barking was an indication of just how well these animals thrived here. The temperature was well below -10 Celsius, not to mention the wind chill, but they were as comfortable as a tourist lying on a sunny beach in the Maldives. The snow crunched beneath his feet as he shouldered the heavy load of his rucksack towards the sled. A thick layer of ice had formed beneath his nose and around his mouth, already attaching itself firmly into the unshaven whiskers of his cheeks.

'Just remember what we spoke about yesterday. Remember your training; keep the dogs in your command and run steady for today. We don't want you to be a hero and end up sledding onto some broken sea ice.'

The words were far from encouraging but Jenson took them on board nonetheless. With a short, sharp 'hep-hep!', he was coasting away from Daneborg under the steam of his dogs in no time. To make life easier, he would follow the tracks created by Wolff's team; that way, he wouldn't need to concern himself with navigation as well as the dogs. He hoped that meant a reduced chance of careering off a fjord or venturing onto some sea ice.

An exhilarating feeling of adventure and freedom struck Jenson as the red buildings of Daneborg grew fainter and were eventually lost to the horizon. Their little red shacks of salvation were now behind them and they would be forced to deal with whatever came their way with what they carried in their sleds. Jenson let out a primal '*wooooohoooooooo!*' as he skated across the earth under the power of his dogs. The sound of the wind and the crunching of ice beneath the sled runners prevented his boyish glee from being heard by Wolff up ahead, while his ski goggles and balaclava masked any facial emotion. He knew the feeling in that moment would last for the rest of his life.

Hours seemed to pass before Wolff pulled up and stopped for a break. His head torch cast a stream of light into the pitch-black air as

Jenson approached, hollering for his dogs to slow and remain calm. His legs were jelly and his body ridged and frozen to the bone but as he squinted past the light on Wolff's head, he saw no such indication of any ailments or discomfort. It appeared the man was at home in these conditions. The frosted air of his breath caught the light and dissipated as quickly as it came.

'Hungry?' Wolff asked Jenson as he trudged over.

'Starving.'

'Remember our training. No matter the circumstances, attend to your dogs first, then yourself.'

Jenson reached into the sled and pulled out the dog food that took up most of what they were able to carry. Only after thanking his dogs and feeding them did he begin to think about opening his flask of hot tea he had prepared that morning. The hot liquid coated his throat as it descended into his stomach. He could feel its warmth radiate outward. It was, by far, the best tea he had ever drunk. Wolff remained quiet as he sat on the sled and ate while perusing the map laid out on his lap. There was little discussion and before long he announced it was 'time to get moving'. Just hours into this expedition, Jenson knew it was going to be a slog. The echoes of his jubilant cries as he set off this morning were now lost to the icy winds and battering of snow that encrusted his frozen face. This was his mission, though, and he tried to concentrate on the task at hand, remembering that people all over the world were relying on him.

Setting up camp that night proved to be a challenge as the wind picked up just as Wolff had signalled that they would stop for the day. The snowdrift was so dense it covered the bottom half of their bodies as they fumbled in the biting cold with flapping guy ropes. Jenson was exhausted, mainly from the unknown feeling of continuous, deep cold that was scorching through his energy reserves. He found it hard not to delve into the next day's rations with his ravenous appetite. Once their tents had been set up, they boiled water to rehydrate their evening meal. Jenson didn't care what the food was, he just needed fuel at this stage of the day. It was surprisingly delicious, although he thought that anything would taste good at this point. The entry vestibule of their tents was opposite each other, so the two of them sat in the doorways of their respective shelters slurping down their rehydrated stew and sharing the odd laugh about Jenson's mishaps throughout the day. He was still an amateur at the sport of mushing, but he surprised the hardened Sirius patroller as to just how quickly he had picked it up. There had been no more line tangles or rogue dogs running off without the rest of their team, or human for that matter.

Jenson made a distinct effort to put the dogs first. He would never rest unless he had first attended to their needs, checking their feet, preparing their food and rubbing their shoulders. It was the temperament required for a good musher, or a soldier. It was a characteristic that had enabled him to take on the responsibility of this mission. There had been Sirius recruits that were less capable than Jenson after six months of training, let alone on their first expedition.

Jenson was fully aware that Wolff knew little of the intricacies of the mission. As far as he was concerned, officers far above his clearance had contracted him as a specialist asset. He could tell that the message had been clear though; this was a mission that reached the very top and the gravity of what was at stake seemed to have the attention of the most powerful international players. For any civilian, the temptation to know more and understand why they were risking their life by escorting a stranger through the harshest of winter conditions would be overwhelming. For a man like Wolff, though, it was just part of the job.

'You did alright today for a white-collar scientist from the city,' Wolff teased as they took in the night sky in their sleeping bags.

Jenson smiled to himself and rejected his label as a white-collar city dweller. He was quite chuffed to be receiving a back-handed compliment from one of the best in the business though.

'Just wait a few days and I'll be the one making tracks for you to follow,' Jenson shot back.

The dogs had finally quietened down, which allowed Jenson and

Wolff to close their tents and get some rest. Jenson was out like a light even with the walls of his shelter being hammered by a blizzard. He didn't envy the dogs outside. They would be constantly fighting the snowdrift and freezing temperatures with nothing but their fur coats and instincts.

Darkness remained the following morning but the sky was luminescent with the captivating display of the northern lights. A liquescence came upon the sky as green lights danced from the horizon. Jenson thought he must've been still dreaming; such was the magnificence of what he was seeing. It was as though the air above them had taken on a new life; a separate realm far away from where they were standing down below. The glow of their headlamps added to the beauty as it lit up their tents in a replicating green glow. Even the dogs were silent as they packed the sleds and harnessed them up for another day of work. Adding to the aura, the wind had abated and the creaks and groans from shifting sea ice was the only sound to be heard. The deep reverberations echoed up from below the ice they were standing on. Jenson just hoped they had drifted too far to the east and ended up on top of the gigantic pieces of floating ice that he witnessed on the flight in. For that moment, he tried to stay in the present and take in every second of the incredible display Mother Nature was putting on. Before long, Wolff came over to indicate they needed to get moving. The mission comes first, *always*, Jenson thought to himself.

The day was relatively stress free, with Jenson slowly gaining more skill and experience from time on the sled. Their existence had been boiled down to sledding, eating and sleeping and by the end of the day they had made good ground. Wolff thought they would be roughly two to three days out from the settlement if the weather held, which he thought it might.

'You can never predict the weather here at this time of year with any certainty but I'm fairly confident we won't get struck down in a blizzard.'

Jenson's body was slowly adjusting to the deep, bone-chilling cold that came with being out in the open in such hostile conditions all day. He was constantly hungry but the rapport he was developing with his team of dogs and with Wolff buoyed him through the lethargy and monotony of the landscape. There seemed to be a mutual respect between the two of them that could be communicated without the need for words. This was fortuitous, considering it was near impossible to talk to one another for most of the day. The weather, physical distance between them and barking of the dogs took any chance of a leisurely chat out the window. By the end of the day, they were often too exhausted to engage in small talk and retired to their sleeping bags shortly after tending to their dogs and then feeding themselves.

As Jenson lay in his tent for the third night, he began to think of what was required once on the ground in the indigenous settlement. His mind had wandered over the past few days and he felt he needed to re-calibrate back to the task at hand. His field notes and data collection were the vital part of the expedition and he needed to ensure his mind was on the ball. If Wolff was correct, and he trusted his judgement with his life, then they would arrive at the settlement tomorrow. Jenson's mind drifted back to the team at Headquarters. He thought about how they were all coping; even Hiram seemed flustered the last time they had spoken. Nya had said to him softly as they were saying goodbye after their conference call that she had never seen him so worked up in all her time under his command. Her soft facial features delicately portrayed a sense of empathy as she spoke with a slight quiver to her usually self-assured tone. There was something about Nya that had captivated Jenson since the time they first met. He felt like an adolescent schoolboy meeting an attractive university lecturer for the first time. Soft dark hair fell over her forehead, cheeks and neck and she had doe eyes that would melt a candle, even in the icy conditions of Greenland. Her intelligence and outlook on the world were impressive, which was also reflected in her professional accolades. She had worked all over the world since graduating from university in Switzerland. Much to Jenson's envy she spoke multiple languages, six in fact; hence her accent. He also thought about Sasha again. She seemed to manifest a presence within his thoughts out of nowhere. It had only been since working with CINS on SK01 that she had entered his thoughts in years. He tried not to read too much into it and instead focused on how he would carry out his data collection tomorrow.

The anticipation made it hard to fall asleep. Despite his fatigue from the physical exertion and biting cold, Jenson was restless and found only fits of sleep through the night. Outside the walls of his tent, a fierce shriek of wind blasted icy flecks of snow and ice. The welfare of his dogs was something he continually thought of. He had no idea how they survived the nights out here. In between the howls of wind and the rustles of dogs, he could hear Wolff snoring, blissfully seeing the night pass by with an uncrowded mind. He then realised that was probably an incredibly presumptuous thought, as he considered all the situations he would've been confronted with in his time with both the Special Forces and Sirius. There wouldn't be a soldier on Earth who doesn't have the memories of something haunting etched into the recesses of their minds.

The morning brought more of what the previous three days had delivered in spades: wind, snow and bitter cold. No matter how much practice Jenson had in packing up the gear, the numbness in his fingers caused him to constantly fumble. It made simple tasks seemingly insurmountable at times. He was thankful for the expertise of his dogs and of Wolff, who had now left Jenson to his own devices most of the time. He figured he was either sick of him or thought he was competent enough to make his own way. He desperately hoped it was the latter.

The sea crashed to their left as they descended the west coast of Greenland's fjords. A wash of icy salt spray coated them from head to toe but the dogs continued to run and run, dragging their convoy of equipment across the undulating wind-swept ice. Deep rumbles reverberated underfoot, signalling the crash of sheets of ice into the sea below. As they edged closer to the settlement, more and more cracks appeared through the ice, creating deep crevasses that halted their progress. Jenson and Wolff zig-zagged back and forth to find a clear path through, often retracing their steps as they came to a wall of ice or dangerous gap that had no way of traversing.

An arduous twelve hours of slogging their weary bodies over technical sections of ice and negotiating sled dogs at the same time finally eventuated to success. Tiny dots resembling houses appeared on the horizon, giving them the motivation they sorely needed to reach the settlement. The exhaustion rooted deep within Jenson's bones seemed to lift slightly as they edged closer. As the sun kissed the horizon on its brief appearance for the day, Wolff and Jenson trudged into one of the shelters. Removing their gear layer by layer to reveal their faces, they were met by stunned looks of a few people mingling around a driftwood table. There was an awkward silence for a moment where nobody seemed to move, and all that could be heard was the soft crackle of the fire and wind buffeting the tiny shack.

'Uh, hello,' Jenson finally uttered, putting up a hand to signal a wave. 'My name is Jenson. This is Wolff.' He signalled towards his guide, standing tall with broad shoulders and steam radiating from his body.

'I hope you don't mind us crashing your party. The weather is really coming down out there!' Wolff said, trying to lighten a confused crowd of locals.

Jenson tried to imagine what the situation looked like from their perspective. It was late in the day and preparations for an evening meal would be the primary thought on their minds. The last thing they would've expected was for two white men to waltz through the door and introduce themselves.

Finally, one of the men rose from a low seat he was crouching on beside the warmth of the fire. He had high cheekbones and a textured olive complexion. His slightly slanted eyes softened the weather-beaten nature of his face by giving him a permanent smile. His hair was jet black and long but tied back in a ponytail that hung loosely behind his neck. His eyes were kind and his teeth white against the dark glow of his skin. He was short in stature but looked strong, with thick arms and legs that had been groomed through a lifetime of physical labour.

He stood before Wolff and looked up at him, extending an arm out to shake his hand.

'Welcome,' he said, embracing Jenson with a handshake as well. 'My name is Tulok.'

CHAPTER 30

Hiram continued to field phone calls from representatives around the world on the progress of his team's findings. It was just past 0900 hours, yet his ear was warm and sore from the telephone receiver. His eyes were slow and tired, struggling to focus on the documents before him and the desire to sleep was becoming overwhelming. There was little good news to provide anyone he spoke to. Nya and Emerson continued to work feverishly at the previous data sets Jenson had collected but their results provided just one conclusion; they were consistent with their previous findings. SK01 was not the usual beast they had dealt with in previous emergencies. This was something of an entirely new entity and could not simply be put into an algorithm to track the potential spread and likely damages. It was looking more and more like the pathology Jenson had hypothesised. In a sense, this was good news, as they hoped to have the data to provide solutions and mitigation measures soon. What was providing Hiram with more trouble was how they would implement those measures. There was no global off switch to prevent civilians from accessing the conveniences of daily life. There was no way to ensure people were aligned with their circadian rhythms to assist sleep and neural regeneration. Ultimately, there was no way that a governing body such as the WHO, the UN or CINS could tell people how to live their lives.

The following day, Nya knocked softly on the door of Hiram's office, her dark hair bouncing loosely over her shoulders. Her brown eyes cast a sympathetic look beneath her glasses as she approached his desk. He looked tired and dishevelled, almost defeated. It was clear that the infiltration of SK01 did not discriminate. Nya would have to move from the role of data analyst on the project to first-hand dealings with a patient. Hiram had succumbed. His usually focused and fierce narrow eyes pleaded with something, anything, for the static and pain in his mind to subside, but for some reason, there was no way to portray that to his protégé standing across the desk. He simply couldn't find the words.

'Hiram.' Nya's voice was gentle and soothing to his ears. 'You and I both know what's happening here.'

Tears welled in the corners of his eyes and the edge of his mouth tremored as he gave a gentle nod.

With the hospital services overwhelmed with SK01 patients, Nya thought there was little point in trying to admit him. Plus, they were possibly on the cusp of identifying that the disease was not communicable but rather a human response to the dramatic shift in way of life. It suddenly occurred to Nya that they had the perfect opportunity to carry out a case study and test the hypothesis that Jenson had suggested. Hiram now had the potential to provide pragmatic, anecdotal evidence to back the claims. It might just be the missing link in the equation of convincing other nations of the proposal.

Her thoughts must have reflected the expression on her face as Hiram looked bleakly up at her from his desk chair and managed to say, 'Do what you need to do.'

It was enough to make Nya wither into a fit of tears but she knew that the time called for strength and resilience. Hiram had proven his character over the long haul and she felt a responsibility to do the same for him in a time of need.

Sitting down next to him, she thought for a moment about what the next move should be. The ubiquity of technology made it almost impossible to escape from nowadays, especially with Hiram's position as director of a nation's intelligence and security organisation. Their office contained some of the most advanced technology in the world and Hiram's apartment contained much of the same equipment.

Nya suddenly recalled a conversation she had with Jenson before he left for the Congo. The captivation she felt while Jenson, this seemingly nonchalant man, unshaven with flowing sandy hair and deep blue-grey eyes, described his house in Capertree. It was devoid of any modern luxuries such as internet, television and other extraneous distractions. He spoke at length about his pot-belly stove, rain on the tin roof at night and the sounds of whip birds that echoed through the canyons and down the cold air of the riverbanks in the early morning and evening. It sounded more like paradise than the home of a world-leading ecologist. She had no way of getting in touch with him at the moment though. He was currently trudging across the frozen waters of Greenland and had no contact with the outside world. There would be no issue in finding the location of the house, it was just a matter of whether he would approve of colleagues he barely knew intruding on his personal life. At this stage, Nya thought, the research would have to take precedence and she had an underlying feeling that Jenson wouldn't mind, given the gravity of the situation.

She contacted the administrators at CINS and was able to obtain Jenson's address and arrange a helicopter for transportation within the hour. An advantage of working for an intelligence agency was the resources available, especially when it was a matter of addressing the health of its director. She informed Emerson of the situation; there was little more they could do at HQ anyway, that was until Jenson sent through the additional data they required.

In what seemed like the blink of an eye, Nya was transporting her mentor and boss to the roof of CINS, where the helicopter awaited to transport Hiram to Capertree. She would accompany him for the foreseeable future; approximately one week, as that was when Jenson was due back in range. It was just days ago that Hiram was presenting the group's latest work at the convention of leaders in Geneva. Now he was almost incapacitated and struggling to collate a coherent sentence.

The skyline of the city grew into a misshapen array of concrete blocks and swirling segments of asphalt. Even the harbour was caressed with a layer of smog haze, stifling the usually photogenic scenery. The streets below were eerily devoid of traffic. Most people had elected to stay home in an effort to reduce the spread of SK01. Nya thought they might be just days away from informing the world that it was all in vain and that the real threat lay hidden amongst modems and their chronic addiction to screens. Before long, the sprawling suburbs gave way to natural bushland and eventually there was nothing but the canopy of trees that blanketed the ground below. Rivers cut deep gorges into the surface of the earth and the air suddenly felt fresh and clean again. She could see why Jenson was so passionate about this area of the world.

The pilot landed in a nearby clearing and as the rotors came to an eventual halt the world around them was transformed. Just like Jenson had described to Nya, the forest came to life with birdsong and the trickle of water in a nearby stream. They entered the house with the assistance of lock-pickers; Nya felt incredibly guilty about breaking into a colleague's house but she reassured herself that they were doing it for the right reasons. The door squeaked open to reveal a humble, small place. There was nothing extravagant about it. The scent of wood that lingered through the place as Nya slowly walked around, the heels of her shoes methodically tapping on the floorboards as she did so. Hiram collapsed into one of the chairs in the corner near the fireplace and began to fade into oblivion in an instant. His energy levels were completely sapped, even the reserve tank that he had called upon so often had left him.

Nya found a stack of wood neatly piled in a nearby shed. She brought a few loads in and began to light the stove to take the chill off the place. It didn't take long before the house felt warm and inviting. By the time the sun was setting over the hills, she was preparing a meal under the glow of candlelight in hope of realigning Hiram's circadian rhythm. It would be a few days before the light-dark cycle would be fully reconfigured, but she hoped its effects combined with the isolation from technology would accelerate his recovery. That was, she thought to herself as she stirred a pot on the stove, if Jenson's hypothesis was correct. She held out hope that it was.

CHAPTER 31

Jenson and Wolff were welcomed with open arms by Tulok after the initial awkwardness of their unexpected arrival dissipated. Beds were cleared for them in an old disused shack with an enthusiasm that left Jenson feeling slightly guilty for their disruption. The shack was primitive at best, with no running water, electricity or plumbing, but the shelter it provided from the howling wind and cold was solace enough for the pair of weary travellers. For Wolff, it provided an opportunity for him to refuel both himself and both teams of dogs. For Jenson, this was the moment he needed to collect valuable data. Over a mug of seal stew that tasted a little like liver, rabbit and fish all mixed into one, Jenson and Tulok had a conversation in broken English about why he and Wolff had suddenly arrived at their doorstep.

'You probably don't know at this stage,' Jenson began, 'but there is an illness that is affecting most of the world at the moment.'

Tulok's eyes widened at the statement but Jenson was quick to reassure him that they were in no danger. 'Because of your isolation to the rest of the world, I would like to make some observations and do some tests over the next couple of days, if you will have us.'

Tulok looked over at his wife who, like everyone else, was clad from head to toe in a traditional Inuit dress. Their coats were made from either walrus or seal skins and lined with the fur of polar bears. Large mukluks covered their feet and thick gloves provided protection for their hands. Jenson and Wolff looked completely out of place in their Gore-Tex alpine gear.

'Will it hurt?' Tulok enquired when Jenson began showing them the neurological equipment used to analyse cerebral activity.

'Not at all. In fact, you won't even know I'm doing anything. The biggest hindrance will probably be me asking you too many questions,' Jenson said with a broad smile. He was finally able to feel his face now the layer of frost had detached from his beard.

The rest of the evening was spent exchanging stories by the fire with multiple refills of seal broth and stew. After a while, the taste seemed to grow on Jenson and eventually, not even the smell seemed to faze him. The warmth it provided was more than enough to convince him that it was exactly what you should be eating in this part of the world. The sheer number of calories in seal blubber was rejuvenating as well. He felt as though he'd burned through most of his energy reserves simply trying to stave off hypothermia.

Time seemed to escape into another dimension, with the darkness and light a seemingly incoherent indicator of what time of day it was. By the time Tulok and his family bid Jenson and Wolff a goodnight, Jenson's cheeks were flushed with warmth and he felt a fatigue that reached deep into his bones. Both Jenson and Wolff were fast asleep within minutes of getting into their sleeping bag.

Jenson woke with cold feet, a frozen nose and no idea what time it was. Naturally, it was dark but that didn't give much of an indicator of night or day. His muscles still ached but he felt as though he'd slept reasonably well and took it on face value that it was probably time to get up. Slipping out of the warmth of his sleeping bag, Jenson looked at the bunk above and found that Wolff was no longer there. The soldier was more acclimatised to the physical load and conditions than he was and was probably occupying himself with the dogs and various other tasks. Jenson had taken some valuable notes already but he was excited to begin extracting more data from the community now he had Tulok's blessing. His first port of call was food, though. The physical labour of dog mushing and intense cold had sapped his energy reserves and after a good night's sleep, he was completely ravenous. Putting on layer upon layer just to walk fifty-odd metres from one building to another was something of a novelty at the moment but he thought it would become tiresome if it was a daily necessity. He then realised that it wasn't just the reality for those who lived here but they may not know anything else. Warmth was a relative term in these reaches of the world.

Entering the main shelter for breakfast, he encountered members of Tulok's family from the night before a few new faces that gawked at him as he clobbered through the icy wooden entrance.

'You slept well?' Tulok asked as Jenson was removing his outer coat. His smooth brown skin was blackened from standing over a cooking fire that was predominantly used for seal and whale blubber. While the acrid smell had become less intense since Jenson first encountered it, there was no escaping its pungent aroma when he stepped inside a shack.

'Like a baby,' Jenson said with a smile. 'Have you seen Wolff this morning?'

Tulok nodded and pointed outside where the dogs were chained. He could see a figure shuffling through the snowdrift amongst the pack carefully attending to each at a time, checking their harnesses and their feet and providing them with sustenance. He felt lazy seeing him out there and suddenly felt as though he had slept in, although he was still unaware as to what time it was. He justified himself with the fact that he had other work to do, something he would need to start straight away.

Over a hot broth at the table with other members of the community, Jenson strategically questioned them about their way of life and the contact they have with the world outside of this frozen wilderness.

'Do you ever leave the community?' he asked as he scraped the bottom of his bowl to siphon the remaining juice. He seemed to be endlessly hungry despite all the food he'd eaten over the past twenty-four hours.

'Sometimes a team will sled into Daneborg for essential supplies we cannot find here or make ourselves. It is a long journey though. Some have never come back.'

'They have died making the journey across?' Jenson asked, almost dumbfounded that anyone would undertake such a feat in this day and age purely for the purpose of restocking supplies.

'Yes.' The man nodded in response. 'We do not have the technology to fly or have motorised sleds. We have dogs, just like you got here. They are the most reliable and cheap to maintain, provide us with companionship and can do a lot of different jobs. Sometimes things go wrong though.'

A heavy silence hung in the air and the background crackle of the fire and soft chatter nearby suddenly became more obvious. The reality of life on Greenland's isolated wilderness suddenly hit Jenson square between the eyes. He made a note in his field book that it was not the absence of stress in communities such as this but it was the nature of the stressor. Perhaps, Jenson thought, the problem was derived from dealing with stressors that the human body is not yet adapted to. Homo sapiens had been dealing with the issue of food insecurity and survival for the entirety of their existence but the mechanisms used to overcome this probably didn't translate to the issues faced today. He sunk a heavy hand into his brow and thought for a moment. The people around him were content; he wouldn't describe them as overtly happy but they were not depressed, anxious or displaying any signs or symptoms of SK01. They had a purpose in life – perhaps it was life itself. It was simple, attainable and it revolved around a common goal with like-minded people. It was also the deep connection with the natural world that reflected what Jenson had recorded in his notes whilst in the Congo. Most decisions about the future of their communities were made with the natural world in mind. They acted in a way that would benefit themselves in the future and ensured their way of life would be prosperous for future generations. An essential element of that was to be frugal with your resources and ensure the environment would be supportive for generations to come.

It seemed to be in direct contrast to the way the rest of the world was heading. The human transformation of the world, purely for the benefit of themselves, had created a lack of primal purpose for the majority of the population. There was also a growing trend in social isolation that dawned upon Jenson as he sat at the table with Tulok, who had joined them for another bowl of broth. The man's short legs fitted snugly beneath the wooden table that they huddled around. He smiled at Jenson before returning to another conversation. There seemed to be a certain aura around him that was similar to that of the Chief in the Congo. It was a gentle respect that was demanded of him when in his presence. Looking out the window to a land of white, Jenson found it inspirational that a community could not only survive in such a hostile climate but do it for so long and thrive at the same time.

The door swung open and Wolff walked through the door. His tall triangular physique blocked the doorway from the icy breeze as he strolled through. Icicles stuck to every aspect of his face that had any hair attached to it. Even his eyelashes had grown extensions in the form of stalagmites. He smiled at Jenson as he walked over to him, causing his cheeks to shed their frozen shell.

'Another lovely day in paradise,' he said, squeezing his frame into the chair beside Jenson. 'It's nice to see you actually doing some work for once.' He pointed towards his notebook where he'd been scribbling for the best part of the morning.

'What do you call the previous four days of dragging a sled across the snow?'

'That's just a matter of survival, Doc. You're doing what you came here for now, yes?' He suddenly turned serious and the smile dissipated from his face.

Perhaps he knew more than he led on, Jenson thought.

'I am. I should finish the neuro testing by the end of today but will need one more day after that to bring it all together and finish my observations.'

'You run the show for now, Doc.' He paused. 'For now.'

CHAPTER 32

A thunderous clap bolted Jenson and Wolff into the upright position, snapping them out of their slumber. The room was pitch black until the sudden ray of light burst into Jenson's retina from Wolff's head torch.

'Fair storm, yes?'

Jenson knew Wolff was smiling, despite not being able to see his face through the onslaught of light from his headlamp.

'Just your usual day in Greenland,' Jenson replied.

They both wiggled back into their sleeping bags but sleep was hard to come by with the thought that the entire shack might blow over at any point. Eventually, after some tossing and turning, and much grumbling from Wolff, they decided the best approach was to get a head start on the day. They would be venturing back to Daneborg once Jenson finalised the neurological readings and uploaded them to a secure data source. The only obstacle standing in their way was escaping the warmth of their sleeping bag and subjecting themselves to another day of bitter conditions. Jenson thought for a moment about Kofi and how he was doing. He chuckled to himself, thinking of how he would react to being thrown into the wilderness of Greenland in freezing temperatures. The man had known nothing else but heat, humidity and vast amounts of dense, green vegetation. Once this was all over, if it was all over, he thought it would be fitting to visit him again. Maybe he would even bring him to Greenland to meet Wolff.

'Fuck it!' Wolff leapt off the bunk and slammed his feet down onto the wooden floorboards and got dressed into his alpine gear in a flash. 'Your turn, Doc!'

Jenson slammed his head back against his pillow as Wolff exited the shack, letting a blast of arctic air in through the door at the same time. The wind continued to howl as Jenson quickly dressed himself from head to toe in merino wool, goose down and Gore-Tex.

After slurping down some breakfast stew and wrapping up his work, Jenson packed his sled while Wolff prepped the dogs for the trip ahead. The wind seemed to have nothing on the sound of two dog teams, eager with anticipation at the thought of mushing for their leaders. The barks and howls prompted the rest of the community's dogs to start as well and in no time, it was so loud Jenson could hardly hear a thing. Tulok came out with a smile on his face and greeted them.

'You are leaving us today?'

Jenson's heart sank with the comment. He had grown close to Tulok and his family since arriving just a few days ago; unprompted and uninvited. He had always found goodbyes a difficult thing to negotiate. Often it was just easier to leave without one.

'We are,' he finally said with a heaviness that barely found its way over the wind and snow. 'I will come inside once the sleds are packed and the dogs are prepped.'

Tulok nodded with a quaint smile and then shuffled away into the white.

'Where's the package?' Wolff shouted to Jenson. 'We can't lose your life's work. My boss would never forgive me for a failed mission with these stakes.'

These stakes? Jenson repeated Wolff's words back to himself. Just how much had this man figured out? And if he had, why wasn't he showing a drop of fear? Those in Special Forces units seemed to possess a neutrality to their demeanour, something they always accounted to their training. Nothing seemed to faze them so long as they fell back on what had been drilled into them time and time again during their selection and training phases.

Jenson passed a chunky black plastic case that contained all the data he'd collected from their time with Tulok and his family. If it got lost, the entire mission was wasted and CINS would be no closer to confirming their hypothesis. He doubled checked the latches were in place before leaving it with Wolff to pack amongst the other scientific equipment. It would be transported with Wolff's team, with the knowledge that he was the more experienced musher and should anything go awry he would have a better chance of saving it than Jenson.

With a solemn trudge, Jenson entered the shack where Tulok and his family were having breakfast. The connection he had formed with them over the past few days despite a language barrier was nothing less than what he had felt in the Congo with Kofi's tribe. His square face beamed with satisfaction as Jenson displayed his gratitude for their hospitality.

'It is not often we get visitors here,' he said with a smile and a brief look out the window to the frozen world that awaited outside.

'I cannot thank you enough. Your generosity means more than you imagine in these circumstances. You have no idea what you may have helped achieve.'

The pair came together in a hearty hug, their bulky jackets hindering a closer embrace. Barking dogs outside prompted Jenson to cut the goodbye short. Wolff seemed eager to get ahead of some weather he thought was coming in. In Jenson's mind, there was always inclement weather here anyway, so a few more minutes would not impede them too much.

'I hope to return one day. It will be then that I can explain what this all meant in a much deeper way, perhaps. For now, all I can say is thank you.'

Jenson waved goodbye to the rest of the family and exited the warmth of the shack into the biting winds of Greenland for another leg of a journey that never seemed to stop twisting and turning. He managed to catch himself before going too far down the path of reflection. There was still work to be done and there were people who were relying heavily on him to complete it, and quickly. He jumped on his sled and gave a thumbs up to Wolff who was parked just ahead. The tightening of the leash sprayed snow into the air and before long, he got the now-familiar feeling of skating across the snow, feeling all its bumps and undulations underfoot and embracing the power of his dogs who desperately wanted to get away; to where, he wasn't sure they knew.

Sections of ice with large crevasses and gigantic moguls reared their heads before too long. Jenson recalled the nerve-racking expedition into the community through this section in pitch-black conditions. Their head torches trying desperately to cut through the snow drift and prevent an incumbent disaster. After several episodes of hauling sleds, gear and dogs over impenetrable walls of ice, combined with many expletives, they entered the ice floes, which provided more open conditions for travelling. By the end of the first day, their progress had been slow but according to Wolff, they would likely make up ground in the coming days.

They set up camp for the evening and thawed their frozen limbs over a cook stove. The remnants of stew Tulok had gifted them on their departure bubbled gently as it defrosted in the aluminium pot. The dogs remained busy, crunching bones and woofing down their meal as well. Once again, there seemed to be no other sound than that of the wind and flecks of ice battering the walls of their tent. If it weren't for the cold, it may have just been heaven on Earth. There were no distractions, no superficialities to drag you into; it was just Jenson, Wolff and their dogs alone on a floating piece of ice. Sleep came quickly to Jenson that night; his bones were tired and he could feel the end of this expedition getting closer. The anticipation seemed to heighten his sense of fatigue, like the marathoner that stumbles in the final kilometres after conquering the previous forty.

The morning presented the worst conditions of the trip thus far. Their tents were half submerged with snow drift and visibility was near zero. Even the dogs had to be yanked from beneath a layer of white powder, whimpering with growing fatigue and cold. Packing up was arduous at best and a nightmare at worst. Jenson was sure something would go missing, as it was impossible to keep track of Wolff let alone all their gear to be loaded on the sled.

'Do you have the package?!' Jenson shouted over the splintering blasts of icy wind.

Wolff gave a thumbs up, which was barely visible. 'I wouldn't leave without it, Doc. It's more important than you now!'

An hour into the day of mushing, Jenson needed a break. His feet felt frostbitten and his hands weren't far off either. His concentration seemed to be waning too and in a moment of reflection, he realised that Wolff was nowhere to be seen. He stopped to listen for his dogs but was left with nothing but the wind in his ears. The white-out conditions had separated them and he had only just realised. How long had he been mindlessly skating across the ice, venturing further and further from Wolff? A panic overwhelmed any sense of rationalisation as Jenson swivelled his head in every direction to see if he could spot anything, anyone. There was nothing but white.

'Wolff! Wolff!' Jenson's words were lost to the wind and the realisation that he was now alone began to settle deep in his gut.

It was then he noticed the haunting sound of moving ice in the distance. They had escaped the treacherousness of crevasses and uneven ice the day before but that had landed them into a false sense of security. They were on the ice floe now and by the deep rumbling underneath Jenson's feet, it was clearly unstable. The lack of visibility only compounded things as there was no way to see how close the ocean was or if he was simply standing on a bobbling iceberg that was drifting further and further away from the mainland. He shouted out to Wolff again. No response. The ice then vibrated and resonated with an eerie sound that was akin to solid steel being slowly bent over itself. Jenson's world suddenly began to close in and the only sound in his head was that of his own heavy breath. His head ached with the cold and his limbs felt like blunt wooden sticks. He was unable to move but knew that he could not remain stagnant. He had a rough bearing to

Daneborg so he knew which direction to travel in a general sense. The only problem was that even if he was just a few degrees off, he would miss the settlement by kilometres. That wouldn't matter anyway, he just realised – Wolff had the data.

'Wollllllffffff!! Fuck! Fuccckkkk!!'

The dogs were getting restless and feeding off Jenson's panic. They began to howl and whimper in alarm that the one who was supposed to be in control was losing it. The ice rumbled and echoed with another deep groan, adding to the unease.

Jenson then made the decision that he would backtrack for an hour, as he worked out that was roughly the last time he had eyes on Wolff. It would be arduous, mentally more than anything, but his hopes of survival and the assurance that the package would find its way to CINS rested on finding him. His head torch strained to cut through the blizzard that raged around him. For the most part, he could only see the flecks of ice mere centimetres from his face that were illuminated by the beam. He was relying heavily on the dogs to negotiate any dangerous sections of ice and he found it hard to believe they could see much as well. The bumps jolted his tired, weak and shivering body as he tried desperately to search his surroundings for any signs of his travelling companion. His voice was hoarse from shouting Wolff's name above the roaring wind. Minutes felt like hours as his fatigue grew to a point it became overwhelming. Hope began to wane; even the dogs were slowing and then they stopped. His limp body gently swayed with the wind as he feebly lashed at the leads to get them going again. They seemed to have set up protest – their fatigue had become too much apparently.

'Hey! Hey!' Jenson yelled as he tried to whip the lead dog into action.

And then he heard it. The distant sound of dogs yelping. Wolff's dogs.

'Wolff!'

He jumped from the sled and feverishly ran towards the sound.

'Wolff!'

'Ryyyyderrrr.'

Jenson stopped in his tracks and strained to hear above his thumping heart and panting breath.

'Ryder. Careful. Crevasse! Crevasse!'

He cautiously inched forward, listening to the crunch of the ice beneath his feet. Jenson's concentration was fixated on the square metre in front of him as he nervously hoped that Wolff was alright.

'Wolff!' he yelled again. 'Can you hear me?'

'Doc. Yes, it's me. I've fallen down a crevasse. I think my dogs are gone.'

'*Fuck.*' Jenson said under his breath. 'Are you hurt?'

There was silence for a while.

'I think I'm okay. Just a bit banged up.'

'And the package?'

'It's with me. The rest is gone though. Dogs, food, gear. All gone.'

Jenson let out a sigh. He wasn't sure if he was relieved or panicked. As long as they had the data, that was all that mattered, he tried to reassure himself.

'Alright, let's get you out of there.'

A distant whimper of a wounded dog echoed up the cold icy crevasse. It would be impossible to get down there and save the dogs as well. He had no idea how far down they were. Fumbling through his sled, he found some rope and an ice axe and got to work setting up an anchor point to belay the safety line down to Wolff. At Wolff's instruction, he dug a ridge line perpendicular to the crevasse and slotted his sled in behind it to act as the anchor. Jenson then sat behind the sled and ran the rope around his waist with the live end thrown down to Wolff.

'You got it?' Jenson shouted down as he positioned himself.

'Let's go!'

Inch by inch, Jenson heaved Wolff's dangling body up the crevasse, pushing firmly against the sled in front of him that was locked in place.

'Good, keep going,' Wolff called out, slightly more audible this time.

Jenson's arms were burning. The man was heavy, especially with all the gear and clothing that he was hanging onto as well.

'Just hang onto that case!' Jenson shouted back with a grunt of effort.

'Couple more metres and we're there.'

Jenson was spurred on by the encouragement and put in an all-out effort. The sled creaked ominously. Jenson stopped, his breath heavy with exhaustion and anticipation. He hoped like hell the sled would hold for just a little longer. Another creak reverberated through his feet. He cautiously gave another pull of the rope. He could almost feel the sled holding on for dear life too. The sled runners were scraping the ice with every point of contact available. Then, it popped. The anchor broke free and catapulted the sled and Jenson forward with the weight of Wolff on the other end. He was now skating across the icy surface and heading straight for the crevasse where Wolff was also plummeting in freefall. Jenson tried anything to slow his momentum, digging his hands and feet into the ice but to no avail. He then felt the ice axe attached to his belt. He quickly pulled it out and jammed it into the ice above his head. Flecks of white powder exploded from the end before it eventually grabbed and jolted him to a sudden stop. The rope tightened around his waist. He held perfectly still for a moment, nervous that any movement would unhinge the grip it had on the ice. He could hardly breathe with the rope constricting his torso and the strain of holding Wolff's weight with mere grip strength. He was clenched in a stalemate battle, unable to lever himself back up the ridge with the fear any movement would dislodge his hold. At the same time, there was no way he could stay idle for too much longer; his arms were killing him as the lactate flooded his forearms and biceps.

Jenson had no idea how long he could hold the position. All he knew was that he had to do something, anything, or they would both end up at the bottom of the crevasse and left to die with the rest of the dogs and their gear. He pulled the rope from around his waist and anchored it temporarily around a ridge of compact ice. The release of pressure from his abdomen brought instant relief. He then worked his way up, using the ice axe to drag his body to the next point of anchor. He would then rest and repeat. It was painstaking work and the progress was slow but he eventually knew he was making headway as the sound of Wolff's voice grew louder.

'You're a genius, Doc!' he shouted from just below the lip of the crevasse. 'A couple more metres and we're there.'

Before long, Wolff's arm appeared and he dragged his battered body onto somewhat solid ground. He was covered in ice and his jacket was ripped from the fall. The exhaustion on his face was muted by his goggles and face mask but as they both lay on the cold frozen ground, there was a knowing look between them that indicated they had just cheated death. Jenson's head sank bank into the sled with utter relief when he saw the square case firmly locked in Wolff's right hand. The mission was still alive and so were they.

CHAPTER 33

Hiram's eyes slowly opened as the sound of a whip bird echoed out from the valley. He had no idea where he was but for the first time in weeks, he felt normal again. He just wasn't sure what had happened and how long he had been out of action. A whistle of a kettle appeared in a nearby room. Curious, he pulled back the sheets from the bed and staggered towards the window. A hazy morning light greeted him as he pulled back the blinds. As his eyes adjusted, he could see nothing but the green of shrubs and trees that were bound by an early morning fog. Dew dripped from the eves outside and light caught the droplets as they hung on a spider's web. The rough-sawn timber of the window frame brushed Hiram's hands as he rested them on the surface. His senses seemed to be heightened; colours were more vivid, smells more intense, sounds more clear. There was a cool scent of forest earth that flooded through the room as he opened the window. A nearby brook gurgled over rock and the sunlight seemed to illuminate the leaves of surrounding trees in a halo. The feeling of awe and sheer presence in the moment was enough to bring a tear to his eye. He was alive.

'You're up.' Nya's soft, distinctive voice was a pleasure to hear.

Hiram smiled as he turned to see her standing in the doorway with a mug of hot coffee in her hand.

'How are you feeling?'

'Good. I feel… really, really good.' Hiram was hesitant at first, still trying to piece together recent events.

'You look well.'

There was a pause before Hiram opened his mouth to speak again. 'Where am I?'

Nya smiled. 'We're at Jenson's place. You were disintegrating back at HQ, showing all the signs and symptoms of SK01. There was nothing more we could do but put Jenson's hypothesis to the test. And I think it's worked.'

Memories flooded back to Hiram. He remembered the feeling of lethargy so intense that he could barely speak or move. It was as though someone was suffocating him and he was slowly losing consciousness. Yet now, here he stood, feeling more rejuvenated than he had felt since childhood. The veil of obscurity had been lifted and he was able to *feel* everything again. He wasn't just a pedestrian watching life from the outside; he felt connected to himself and to everything around him again.

'Jenson,' Hiram uttered under his breath.

'He's still in Greenland,' Nya reassured him.

'He's done it.'

'Maybe. Maybe.' There was a cautiousness to her tone. 'You're just a case study at this point. We're going to need more data to back up our claims if we want to implement something more broadly. Hopefully, when he returns, that evidence will be available.'

Hiram looked over at Nya and simply smiled. 'He's done it.'

'C'mon, you must be starving. I'll fix you some breakfast.'

The wooden floorboards accentuated their footsteps as they walked to the kitchen. It was alive with the smell of fresh bread toasting and coffee brewing. It created a warmth to the room that contrasted with the early morning chill outside. The kitchen led into an open-planned living area where a leather couch flanked the room and a wooden table setting sat idle in the middle. A few photographs decorated the walls, most of them depicting a beautiful landscape such as waterfalls, a stretch of beach or mountain range. A large window opened the space to the outside world, where tall trees stood majestically beside a riverbank. The morning fog was slowly lifting with sunlight filtering through the canopy of green. The air was rich with moisture left by the chill of night and flowed freely through Hiram's lungs. Sitting down on a balcony step, he watched a robin flicker from branch to branch in staccato movements, chirping occasionally to a nearby friend.

Nya came out with a plate of toast and jam and a coffee in the other hand. She sat down next to him and placed the breakfast to one side.

'Beautiful, isn't it?' she said as they both gazed out to the forest before them.

Hiram simply nodded and took a sip of his coffee.

'What's the latest from HQ?' he asked after some silence had passed.

'That's not for you to worry about at this point. We'll need you healthy for the next stage of this process.'

'When's Jenson back from Greenland?'

'We're not sure specifically but we will have word the moment he reaches communications and sends the latest data through. After that, it will be a matter of hours, maybe a day, before he's back.'

There seemed to be no resistance from Hiram in Nya's stance that he needed to stay right where they were for the time being. Although he felt healthy again, there was a lingering fear that the moment he returned to HQ, he would fall straight back into the grips of SK01 once again.

CHAPTER 34

'You should never do that to me again, you bastard!' Jenson shouted as he dragged Wolff completely free from the entrapment of the crevasse. He smiled as he rested his head down on the ice and let out a relieved laugh.

'We're not out of the woods yet. We lost our best dogs and most of our gear down that fucker.' He chucked a hand full of snow down in frustration.

Jenson thought of the connection he had observed between Wolff and his dogs. They were almost an extension of his family, the way he treated them. Tulok's family was the same. They weren't just a resource that provided an essential part of survival out here, they were companionship as well. The pain on Wolff's face grew more intense as the realisation set in that he was alive but his dogs remained, likely dead, at the bottom of a crevasse. There wasn't much Jenson could do to provide consolation. He simply reached out and placed a hand on his shoulder.

The pair of them sat there for a time in the driving wind and cold without a word being spoken. Wolff then gingerly rose to his feet and let a hand out to Jenson to do the same. The freezing conditions had stiffened his joints, which ached and creaked as he stepped to his feet. The remaining dogs huddled amongst each other by Jenson's sled. Wolff trudged towards it and placed the case in amongst their remaining gear and motioned for them to get going. There was nothing quite like dog mushing in the arctic to numb your sense of pain.

Now they were down to just the one sled and team of dogs, it made life a little more difficult for the journey home. One of them was forced to perch themselves on top of the sled amongst the gear while the other drove. Inevitably, this ended up being Jenson most of the time, as Wolff was the more experienced musher of them. It was a precarious position that required little movement, so the chill of the air seeped its way through every layer of clothing without a buffer from body heat generated through physical work. He was also at risk of being bounced off when they encountered technical sections of ice. Compounding it all was the fact the dogs now had to pull extra weight and knew something was awry after earlier events. Multiple stops were necessary, progress was slow and the conditions were worsening. Jenson's hands and feet were succumbing to frostbite and the incessant shaking from the cold slowly subsided. His body was hypothermic and gradually shutting down bodily functions one at a time.

By the end of the day, they were both exhausted, as were the dogs. Setting up their tents was an ordeal once again in blustering freezing conditions and was only made worse by Jenson's numb and blackened fingertips and toes. Fine motor skills became near impossible to complete simply due to the lack of feeling in his fingers. They had covered less than half the distance they set out to that day and had spent more than their fair share of energy getting there. After feeding the dogs and then themselves, a silent Wolff retreated to his sleeping bag and Jenson soon followed, his body aching and cold but somehow unable to find rest or get warm. All that Jenson could think of was how close he came to being out here alone, without any evidence of his data capture for what the mission set out to achieve. The whimper of a half-dead husky haunted his mind as he closed his eyes in an effort to sleep. The pain Wolff was feeling at the same time was beyond Jenson's scope at this stage. He could only liken it to losing a family member.

Morning provided little respite from the wind and cold as they packed up and set off for another arduous day. The exchanges between

Wolff and Jenson had disintegrated into gestures and single syllables; any effort to conserve mental, physical and emotional energy. Fatigue was constant and thanks to the bulk of their food supplies being lost down a crevasse, the pang of hunger was now a lingering companion as well. The dogs were also showing signs of exhaustion. They were dragging weight that was beyond what was expected and operating on little food. The only thing working in their favour was the fact they were built for this environment. The white cold stretches of ice were home for them. Jenson, on the other hand, had never felt more isolated, alone and scared in his life. It wasn't necessarily the fear of losing his fingers and toes or even his life. It was the feeling that if he and Wolff didn't make it back to Daneborg, he was letting down millions, perhaps billions, of people who were depending on him. That feeling was enough to make him sick to his core.

Jenson could tell that Wolff's concentration had heightened after the events of yesterday. There was a determination to ensure the loss of the dogs meant something; that their sacrifice and loyalty were not lost in vain. He knew he would be hungry, exhausted and in pain from the injuries he sustained in the fall. But he was a military man at heart. His training would take over.

The mission had brought them closer together, perhaps closer than Wolff had wanted. But in the time they had spent together, Jenson could see the transformation in Wolff unfold. There was now an understanding of the sheer enormity of the task at hand. Wolff had only been briefed on the skeleton components of the mission. It was simple for him – lead two teams of dogs with a foreign doctor to the isolated settlement down south and make sure to return. The field notes stressed that no matter the circumstance, he was not to let anything happen to Dr Jenson Ryder. It was incomprehensible for most to understand that the fate of so many rested in the hands of one man, but Jenson could see the realisation was now setting in.

Wolff had openly berated himself for not being more aware of the danger of crevasses in the section of ice they were crossing at the time of their fall. He had been hounding Jenson to be aware of the dangers of sea ice more than anything else. There had been several close calls over the journey when they had ventured on to ice floe. It had the potential to lead them astray and trap them on the open water indefinitely. The focus on sea ice had meant they were more complacent with other inconsistencies. Sounds went unheard, changes in the texture of the snow went unnoticed, their minds justified the anomalies they encountered. There was little point in dwelling though. Their focus had to shift to what was before them.

Jenson was perched uneasily at the front of the sled as they battled their way through the headwinds and scathing blizzard of icy snow. He had barely moved in fear of falling off or tipping the sled again. It had already happened several times before, scattering the contents of the sled, including the package, across the ice. It left them scrambling to retrieve everything before it was buried in snow drift. When it had happened twice in as many minutes, they both knew it was time to stop, take stock and rest for a while. They still had a long way to go but they risked never arriving in Daneborg alive if they continued to battle on in these conditions. Wolff halted and jumped off the driver sled to walk towards Jenson. He shuffled gingerly a grimace spread across the exposed elements of his face.

'C'mon, we need to get you warm.'

'And you are?' Jenson replied, managing a hint of sarcasm.

'Far from it. But we've got a while to go today; we can't have you getting hypothermic.'

Jenson already felt hypothermic. In fact, he had felt a coldness that stretched to his bones the moment he arrived in Greenland all that time ago in shorts and a shirt from the Congo. The look on the face of their driver as he slammed the car door shut and shivered in desperation to get warm brought a smile to his face.

'Hot soup, that's the ticket to happiness out here,' Wolff said as he rummaged through a drybag.

'I didn't think we had any left.'

'I always have a few tricks up my sleeve, Doc.'

The two of them sat in a tent they had quickly set up, huddled close to each other to try and warm themselves as they slurped on soup. Jenson had no idea what was in it but it was by far the best soup he had ever consumed in the entirety of his life. He could feel the hot chunky liquid cascade down his throat and into his belly, radiating from the inside out.

'I think I needed this,' Jenson said, breaking a long silence.

'I know.'

By day's end, they had started to make progress as the storm abated. Jenson was thankful for the experience of Wolff in making them stop halfway through the day. He didn't think he would have hands or feet left if they decided to push on. As he looked up to the horizon, a smattering of green light began to flow across the sky. Almost in a sign of reassurance, the beauty of the northern lights made themselves known to the pair of weary travellers once again. The boost it gave to Jenson's morale was more than he could've imagined and for the first time in days, he managed to fall asleep in minutes, not hours.

Another forty-eight hours had passed, yet there was still no sign of Daneborg on the horizon. Jenson was beginning to have feelings of doubt. Would they ever make it back? Were they lost? Had they been walking to an incorrect bearing all this time and overshot the town? The only reassurance he had was the fact he was travelling with an expert in this area of the world. Wolff would never get lost out here, Jenson thought to himself, as the dread in his stomach grew deeper. He had Special Forces training, he had been a Sirius patroller for a decade and was by far the most experienced man for this job. For now, that's all Jenson could hang his hopes on. The cold continued to nag away at him. He'd managed to stall the progress of frostbite but the fatigue seemed to grow exponentially with each passing hour.

The constant buffering of the wind and ice would be taking a toll on Wolff too. He wondered whether a smattering of doubt had crept into his mind. Their progress had been slow after the incident days earlier at the crevasse, but there was a growing unease that they should be in Daneborg by now. They stopped for a moment to take stock. Jenson sat motionless in the sled, too cold to even turn his head and ask what was happening. Wolff took a compass reading and double-checked his maps. North-North-East, they were on course.

'What's the issue?' Jenson shouted from ahead.

'Just some readjustments. Some buckles coming loose.'

Jenson sensed immediately he was lying. Doubt had begun its insidious creep into both their minds. The wind blew hard into Jenson's face, his cheeks brutalised by splinters of ice. There was nothing more to do at this point than to push on and hope they hadn't overshot the mark.

'Are you sure we're on the right track?' There was a wavering tone to Jenson's question.

Silence ensued as Wolff gathered what was left of their belongings and retied them onto the sled, trying to mould his actions to the lie he'd told moments earlier.

'Wolff?'

'Yeah, Doc, we're fine. Just some readjustments, like I said. We'll be underway in a minute. Sit tight.'

Wolff stuffed the maps back into his jacket pocket and took one last look down at the compass.

'North-North-East,' he said under his breath.

With the snap of the reins, the dogs swung into action and began hauling the load once again. Jenson jolted back into his nest within the sled and the mind-numbing journey continued.

The night was a restless one for both Jenson and Wolff. Doubt sat deep in their guts, stewing and festering the hope that had propelled them through adversity so far. The silence between them was the result of neither one knowing that the other was just as concerned about their current situation. If they didn't reach Daneborg by end of the tomorrow, there was clearly something awry. They had either strayed off course due to an incorrect bearing or had ventured onto an ice floe that had separated them from the mainland. Jenson hoped like hell that it wasn't the latter. Ice floes could be as large as a country and it would take days before they could navigate their way to solid ground, if at all. There was also the chance they could be stranded on the floe until it was pushed back by the ocean currents towards the mainland. He tried to ease his mind with the thought that he was with the most capable man for this scenario. Wolff's exploits in this part of the world were exemplary, yet that knowledge did little to ease his racing mind.

Jenson woke to the whining of dogs; their hunger and exhaustion were crippling their spirits as well. All of them had lost significant weight over the past few days. The loss of their food, and their own for that matter, had not just taken a toll physically but was draining their mental fortitude as well. There was one anomaly as Jenson adjusted his eyes to a dull grey morning light inside his tent. There was no wind. Finally, Jenson thought, they might get some favourable conditions. This could be the break they needed to run the home stretch back to Daneborg. Unzipping the tent revealed a horizon that was hugged by the faint glow of the sun, its light reflecting an incredible array of blues. Blocks of sculptured ice caught the light as though they had been placed there deliberately.

'Finally a decent day, Doc.' Wolff's head poked out the neighbouring tent with a smile.

'I never thought I'd see the day.'

Following a scant breakfast of something Jenson didn't care to know the contents of, they were underway for another day. The lack of wind cleared the air for a crispness to settle around them. It was something he had felt when first arriving in the country. The lack of humidity in the air combined with the freezing temperature created a stimulant that was far stronger than any drug Jenson had ever encountered. There was no time required to wake up in the morning. You opened your eyes and felt like you had been slapped across the face with a cold wet rag. The lack of snowdrift made the going easier for the dogs as well and they seemed to be making progress. Even Wolff seemed cheerier.

'These are the days you live for, Doc!' he shouted from behind as he steered the dogs through a tricky layer of ice. 'You're hungry, you're tired but you don't give a shit because you're out here!'

Wolff's comment stirred Jenson's thoughts again. The more he thought about his hypothesis, the more he thought he was on the right track. Wolff was right. When your needs are boiled down into the bare necessities of life, nothing else matters. The highs are high and the lows are low but there is no time to linger in one or the other. You simply take what's thrown your way. If someone were to look down in observation of what he and Wolff had been doing the past ten days, they would see two lonely and isolated men navigating between two points. At night they would set up their tents, eat and take care of their animals. The next day they would do it all over again. It sounded monotonous and pointless. Jenson then thought about the identical observation of someone living in a city. They would wake up, sit in their car then sit at their desk, say goodbye to people they barely spoke to during the day and sit in the car to return to their home. They would eat something and go to bed. The next morning would see a repeat of those events. The difference between the two scenarios was primarily based around location and movement. They were isolated out on the Greenland ice sheets but they were far more immersed in their daily activities and far more active in their pursuits. Somehow, Jenson thought, he needed to provide that perspective to HQ so they could relay it in the presentation of their findings. He had anecdotal evidence from the Congo and south-eastern Greenland but was anxious at the prediction that it would simply be insufficient to implement change.

As the faint glow of the sun tried desperately to creep over the horizon and warm the frozen bodies of Wolff, Jenson and the dogs, it suddenly dawned on Jenson that he hadn't had contact with the outside world for some considerable time. He didn't know what the status of SK01 was. Was Abel still in Nuuk waiting to hear from him? He was long overdue from the ETA they had provided. He didn't even know if there would be anyone left at HQ. The mystery illness could've captured them all by now. He and Wolff could well be two of a dwindling world population. The thoughts depressed him, so he directed them towards something else. He thought of Nya. There was something about her that captivated him. Her mystique, her worldliness and demeanour were impressive. Sasha also crossed his mind again. He wondered if she had been taken hostage by SK01. Again, his thoughts took a dark avenue that was only arrested when the sled suddenly stopped.

'There she is, Doc!'

In the distance, a long way in the distance, the tiny red shacks of Daneborg could be seen perched atop a white stretch of earth. Relief overcame them both and Jenson, elated at the sight, jumped out of the sled and gave Wolff a bear hug. They were going to make it. Wolff laughed and slapped Jenson heartily on the back with a broad smile emerging from beneath the protective layers of clothing.

'I didn't think you were worried,' Jenson said after they had calmed down and composed themselves again. '"Just some readjustments", if I recall correctly?'

'Never in doubt, Doc. Never in doubt,' he replied with an opaque smirk. 'C'mon, let's get warm and fill our bellies.'

Jenson hopped back into the sled. The dogs, sensing their master's hope and anticipation, pulled hard at the reigns and set off at breakneck speed. Suddenly, the biting cold seemed less of an inconvenience and the white, frozen landscape took on a new light. It was amazing what rose-tinted glasses could do to your perspective, Jenson thought to himself as felt to his right once more to check the package was still safely in his possession. He would need to get the data off to Abel as soon as they got to Daneborg. Food and warmth would have to wait.

More than four hours passed before the pair of battered travellers slid into Daneborg. The dogs were thanked tirelessly as they hopped off the sled. Once again, Jenson realised the importance of these animals in this environment. There was no question that without them, if both teams had been lost down that crevasse, they wouldn't be standing where they were right now. Aster came out from one of the shacks to greet them.

'You made it. I was beginning to think you had taken up ranks at the settlement down south.' He then looked around in confusion. 'Where are the other dogs?'

'We had a run-in with a crevasse. I'm lucky to be standing here. The dogs and half our gear weren't so.'

Aster's face turned to a grimace as he looked at the ground and shook his head in disbelief. It was clear he was also close with the team and found it difficult to compute the news.

'I need you to focus, Aster. We have to get these dogs fed and this gear unloaded before the weather turns on us again.'

The apprentice quickly snapped out of his depression and began unleashing the dogs and took them away to the pens. Jenson gave a confused look over to Wolff.

'The weather?' he asked. 'It's the best we've seen in days. You think it's changing again?'

Wolff shook his head. 'A soldier needs tasks to keep his mind from wavering.'

With that thought in mind, Jenson picked up the package and raced inside to begin the transfer. The drone method they had used in the Congo wasn't feasible with the conditions out here. Plus, the distance was far too great for their drone to travel from Daneborg to Nuuk. He would have to compress the files and send them to Abel using the Sirius computer. Naturally, their technology wasn't up to the standard used at CINS and would take some time. It was imperative that Jenson started the process immediately so Abel could receive the files as soon as possible. As far as he knew, he would be waiting eagerly in Nuuk to receive it. He just hoped that was still the case. His numb fingers fumbled with the keyboard and his brain struggled to switch into the 21st century. He had spent days undertaking the most innate and primitive of tasks of travelling from point A to point B. Despite the relatively simple layout of Daneborg, there was still an element of culture shock that was washing over Jenson as he held his breath watching a progress line slowly move across the screen in front of him.

It seemed to move at an agonising speed; even the ice encrusted in his beard was beginning to melt at a faster pace.

'Has the package been sent?' Wolff stood in the doorway removing the outer layers of his clothing, his enormous frame dwarfing the scale of the shelter. 'My apologies for our ancient technology. We don't tend to need much more than email and the occasional weather information out here.'

'The way it should be,' Jenson replied with a smile.

Moments later, the smile on Jenson's face grew wider as he received confirmation from Abel that he had received the data and was organising his extraction from Daneborg as soon as weather permitted. It then suddenly dawned on him that he would be saying goodbye to Wolff, perhaps for good. There was no way of knowing if he would see the man again after this. Despite their hardships, or perhaps because of them, they had developed a close relationship. A melancholy washed over him as the reality of the situation sank in. It had been the same with Kofi as well. They had experienced and achieved so much together and leaving that bond behind was a crushing blow to Jenson's demeanour.

'Congratulations, Ryder. The mission is complete.' Wolff shook his hand while the other cradled a hot cup of coffee. The aroma was enough to make Jenson feel warm again.

CHAPTER 35

Nya's voice took on a tone of optimism as she spoke on the phone. Hiram had been listening intently, trying to pick up on what was being said. He felt a duty to get back to CINS and implement a strategy to contain SK01. Never had he had to step away from his role as Director as a result of personal circumstances. He long considered such a thing a weakness and pushed himself to be seen as the man who could achieve anything he set his mind to. However, Nya had been steadfast in her decision that he was to remain at Jenson's place until further word of the expedition in Greenland. Deep down, he knew she was right.

'Fantastic news. Thank you, Abel. We'll see you soon.'

Hiram's eyes lit up. It was clearly Abel relaying positive news regarding Jenson's status. He stood in anticipation, eagerly waiting for Nya to divulge the contents of the conversation.

'So?' he prompted.

'Jenson completed the expedition. Abel has the data and is extracting Jenson from Daneborg as we speak.' Her voice was calm and controlled, trying in vain to contain Hiram's eagerness.

A smile came across his face. 'Let's get back to HQ. We have work to do.'

Nya was clearly reluctant by the look on her face. She remained protective of Hiram, knowing that his health was key to alleviating the devastation caused by SK01. If they lost their leader altogether, the hope of implementing a global mitigation strategy was significantly reduced.

'I'm fine. Look at me,' Hiram reiterated as he stood before Nya in Jenson's kitchen.

There was a silent pause where even the birdsong from outside seemed to quieten in anticipation of Nya's decision. Hiram found it slightly humorous that Nya had ultimate control of the situation despite the hierarchy of CINS. It appeared that the moment he had exited HQ in an incapacitated state, he relinquished all power of leadership.

'Okay,' she finally uttered under her breath. 'I'll arrange transport back to CINS. But the moment you start to show any symptoms of SK01, we're taking you straight out of there. Understood?'

Hiram nodded in recognition of her demands but the smirk remained on his face. He was excited to finally get on top of this beast that had taken the world over. The task suddenly seemed somewhat manageable; that was if the data confirmed their hypothesis. The two of them quickly cleaned the place up to ensure Jenson's home was left as they found it.

The tranquillity of their surroundings was suddenly overcome by the roar of helicopter rotors descending to the ground nearby. The tree canopy heaved violently with the turbulence as the transportation team from CINS touched down. A shift came over both Hiram and Nya as they walked with their heads ducked for safety towards the helicopter. The doors shut behind them as they climbed aboard and put their headsets on. As quickly as the peace and harmony of the place had been upheaved, it returned once again as the helicopter went skyward. By the time it was out of earshot, it was as though they were never there. The river continued to flow, the birds continued to sing and ants continued to forage on the damp forest floor.

Emerson was waiting for them as they touched down at HQ. He had received the data from Abel and was running preliminary analysis but indicated that the results looked to be promising so far.

'Everything I have done so far seems to support Jenson's proposal.'

The three of them raced down the dimly lit stairwell to the lab space. Hiram's sense of anticipation was growing by the step. They entered the cool white space of CINS HQ where screens dotted the walls and followed Emerson to a computer where a complex array of numbers and graphs depicted little to the untrained eye. To Emerson and Nya, however, there were flecks of gold. Littered throughout the numbers were signs that showed a clear and distinct correlation between SK01 readings and those from Greenland and the Congo.

'You see the difference here?' Emerson pointed at a particular column of recordings on the screen before them. 'That is the data just received from Greenland. It's exactly the same as the readings from the Congo and supports Jenson's observations as well. There seems to be a correlation between exposure to artificial light sources and SK01 cases and an inverse relationship to time spent in contact with the natural world.'

Nya and Hiram looked intently at the screen.

'Best of all,' Emerson continued, 'there is a statistically significant correlation between the disruption in circadian biology and SK01 cases and that significance is completely abated in the cases from Greenland and the DRC.'

The information sank in for a moment before Hiram started to think of his next move. If this was enough proof, and it would need to be, then he needed to present the findings to other national security agencies ASAP.

'Would you say this is conclusive evidence?' Hiram asked after a period of silence.

'It's certainly not completely concrete but it's something. We've been fishing for answers to this for far too long now. If we don't take action on this, even if it's incorrect, it would be extremely negligent from a government agency such as us.'

Emerson's words sunk in as they stood before his computer screen. Hiram would need to be careful as to how this information was relayed to others. It could cause rapid upheaval should it enter the hands of the general public; even in the hands of some governments. He paced back and forth as Nya and Emerson continued to trawl through the mounds of data before them. When they looked around moments later, he was gone.

Hiram had entered into full swing when Nya finally located him in his office. He was on a phone call with their British counterparts, explaining the findings and potential implications.

'We need urgent action. I am proposing an immediate meeting of the world's security agencies to flesh out a plan.'

He looked up to see Nya at his doorway. The gentle calmness that she had seen enter his mind had recessed and his eyes now portrayed that of pure focus and determination.

'I have a man on the ground in Greenland who is due for extraction. We can get his perspective once we meet and I assure you it will make more sense.'

There was a continued back and forth between the other parties on the phone before Hiram was finally able to convince his colleagues to attend a meeting in forty-eight hours in Geneva. He hung up and placed his fists on the desk in front and took a deep breath. His shoulders collapsed with relief at the realisation that the first step was in place.

'What's the latest on Jenson?' Hiram asked Nya, who continued to stand at the door of his office with a concerned expression across her face. 'We need him in Geneva for this meeting.'

'I'll follow up with Abel.'

CHAPTER 36

Abel stepped out of the helicopter and onto the frozen ground beneath him. As always, he was impeccably dressed in a black suit and tie, which fluttered in the turbulence of the rotors above. The man that approached him seemed unrecognisable. Beneath the beanie and snow goggles, an unkempt blonde beard supported a leaner face than usual. Wind-chapped lips were concealed under encrusted ice around his face and he seemed to have grown taller or at least had the perception of being so.

'I never thought I would say this but it's good to see you, Abel.'

'Likewise, Dr Ryder. I'm glad to have you back safe and sound.'

A subdued handshake was all that reflected their relief at seeing one another before they walked towards the helicopter and climbed in. In a matter of moments, the tiny Sirius outpost was nothing but a mere speck on the vast ice sheets of Greenland's east coast. An incredible sense of sadness crept up on Jenson as he peered down from the cockpit. That speck had changed him as a human being. The sheer rawness of the experience he shared with Wolff was more than an adventure or a tall tale of escape. It was existence pared back; nothing extraneous, nothing unnecessary. The emotion of the experience washed over him as they banked west and headed for Nuuk. Over the intercom, Abel informed him that there was more to be done once they landed.

'I'll fill you in on the finer details once we're back in the hotel but we need you in Geneva in the next thirty-six hours.' His voice crackled through the headset and struggled to compete with the sound of the engine.

Jenson acknowledged the information with a subtle nod of the head and continued to look out at the landscape below. The sun tried its best to break the barrier of the horizon and cast a deeper shadow across the ice. A faint reflection was all that could be managed but the effect was a silky orange glow that shimmered back at them as they moved swiftly above. Ice melted from his beard and dripped onto his lap. It would be nice to be warm for once, Jenson thought as he struggled to hold the sadness at bay. He had forgotten what it was like to be truly warm since arriving in Greenland over two weeks ago.

The hotel staff gave Jenson a curious look as he checked in alongside Abel. They were certainly the odd couple in the way they were dressed. Jenson still had all his expedition gear on, decked out from head to toe in merino, goose down and Gore-Tex. The reflection he had glimpsed of himself in the lobby even gave him a slight surprise. He chuckled to himself as he went upstairs to his room with Abel on his left, slender and sleek in his Italian wool suit.

Placing his bag on the bed, he sat down alongside it and let out a deep sigh.

'Have a shower and a hot drink and then I'll brief you on the next move,' Abel said as he went through the door to his adjoining room. 'Maybe a shave too.'

Jenson smiled and nodded in agreement. If his inclinations were correct, he would be presenting the findings of his research to a powerful group of government officials. It was probably best to not look like a caveman in that scenario, so he shuffled to the bathroom in search of a razor and shaving cream. He turned the faucets of the shower and waited for the water to heat up. Before long steam filled the shower and he stepped in. An almost foreign filling washed over his body as he submerged his head under the silky warm water. He opened his eyes to look down at the blackened tips of his toes and fingers. He knew little about frostbite but hoped he wouldn't lose anything as a result. He inspected the middle finger on his left hand as it was clearly the worst of them all. The fingertip was blackened down to the lunular of his nail and had little feeling, if any at all. The rest of his limbs had escaped with stage one frostbite and looked more like a burn than anything else. Most of his toenails were gone and as he slowly regained the feeling from his core to extremities, pain throbbed through his entire body. Drowsiness and lethargy like nothing he had experienced before overwhelmed him to the point where he had to turn the shower off in fear he might collapse under the soothing warm water. He got out and went straight to bed. The clean hotel sheets felt odd after huddling inside an increasingly pungent sleeping bag each night. His head sank deep into the feathered pillow and in an instant, his eyes were closed, his breathing deep and his conscious mind vacant.

'Dr Ryder. Dr Ryder. Wake up, we have much work to do,' Abel said, his usual calmness lost for a moment.

Jenson eventually opened his eyes, unsure where he was. The confusion must have shown upon his face as Abel reassured him that he was in fact back in Nuuk and not in the middle of the North-East Greenland National Park.

'We need you up and ready for a flight to Geneva soon and I am yet to brief you,' Abel said in a usually hurried tone.

Jenson's aching body struggled to remove the covers of the bed and get him to an upright position. His head felt heavy, almost like he had a hangover. Before he could reacquaint himself with his surroundings, Abel launched into his briefing notes. He would be on a flight to Geneva that was scheduled to depart from Nuuk at 9.30 p.m. tonight; it was already 4.00 p.m. The meeting was called by Hiram to consult with other government security agencies and present the findings of their research, just as Jenson had suspected. Abel was puzzled that Jenson was yet to enquire what the analysis had revealed. As he handed him the summary notes, he simply nodded and smiled in recognition. He seemed to already know the answers that lay before him on the page scribbled with notes, tables and graphs.

'Nya and Emerson have done a good job at collating the research in such a short time,' he eventually said as he handed back the papers to Abel.

Jenson was to accompany Hiram to the meeting to provide context, clarity and a backbone to what he would present to the other leaders.

'Am I to wear a white coat and glasses?' Jenson asked in jest as he contemplated his place at the table with everyone else.

Abel didn't take the bait and continued to provide more and more information on each of the delegates that would be attending. Everything from their political standing to their family life had been documented in the folders before them. The information became overwhelming eventually and the deep feelings of lethargy had returned. He was almost looking forward to the flight; at least it would give him a chance to sleep – another perk of being on a private plane.

After almost an hour of talking and handing folder after folder to Jenson, Abel finally stopped.

'Are you ready?' he asked.

Jenson simply nodded his head and climbed back to bed.

CHAPTER 37

Nuuk airport was as Jenson remembered when they first arrived: cold, bleak and noisy. The earth seemed to be darker in this part of the world, even at night. Rain hammered down on the tarmac as they were escorted to the plane. Jenson gave a wry smile as he remembered the same journey to the airport from the plane when they arrived from the Congo. He had more appropriate clothing this time around. Ironically, it was the same man who was driving the cart.

'You found yourself some warmer clothes this time, eh?' He laughed.

'I didn't think I'd survive long in shorts and a t-shirt.'

A jet splintered the grey sky above them as they bordered their aircraft. A flutter of ravens protested at the squall it created in their air space. In a matter of moments, Abel and Jenson were on their way to Geneva, ready to convince the world's leaders of their research and ideas. For the first time since arriving back from Daneborg, the task seemed a little daunting. How would he and Hiram convince the world that they would need to drastically overhaul the way they lived to prevent SK01 from strangling the entire human race? The thought was too big to process and Jenson was still weary from the expedition, too weary to contemplate such an enormous undertaking.

For now, he shelved the thought and concentrated on getting some more rest, food and perhaps a whisky or two. The plane seemed to be more luxurious than he previously remembered it to be. Every detail was considered – leather lining, curved edges, soft-close doors and cupboards and intricate warehousing of anything that had the potential to break. He sat in a seat by the window and observed the world passing below him at several thousand metres. They were already heading over northern Europe and tiny patches of light drifted up from the ground, indicating the presence of cities. *Would that now become a thing of the past?* Electric light clearly had a part to play in all of this. He rubbed his hands through the wiry, coarse hair of his beard and tried to switch off.

Jenson was woken again by Abel shaking his limp body, this time in the plane seat with his head rested against the window. He had somehow slept through the entire landing process and was surprised to see solid ground just metres below them as he peered out the window. He looked bleary-eyed up at Abel who must have seen the confusion on his face.

'We're here, Dr Ryder. We've landed in Geneva. It's time to meet with Hiram and prepare for the congregation.'

Without a word, Jenson stood up and began walking down the softly lit aisle of the plane to the exit and onto the tarmac. *Another country*, he thought as his feet touched the ground. It was warmer than Greenland but was hardly a balmy day. An icy wind swept across the open fields of the airport and a fine mist clung to his face. Grey skies masked the sunshine and clearly the spirits of the ground crew as well. Their solemn faces showed little emotion as they worked with typical Swiss efficiency, unloading the bags and equipment from below.

The hotel provided some respite from the cold and wintery conditions outside. A white marble floor encompassed the lobby area where a wooden desk sat perfectly centred. A tall man with a bald head was checking in as Jenson and Abel approached.

'Jenson?' the man said with a soft smile. It was Hiram.

Dressed in his typical grey suit that was impeccably fitted, he looked as sharp as always. Jenson would never have guessed that he had succumbed to SK01 if Abel hadn't told him in their briefing. They talked like old friends while the hotel receptionist organised their room keys and finalised details. Despite the short time they had spent together, Jenson felt a distinct connection with Hiram similar to what he had felt with Kofi and Wolff. The comradery that developed when working through adversity to achieve a common goal was more powerful than either of them could ever have imagined.

'Get settled and then we'll discuss our approach over dinner. Sound good?'

Jenson nodded in agreement. The elevator shut with a soft ding and shot them up to the top of Geneva's most prestigious hotel. Even the inside of the elevator seemed luxurious to Jenson as he studied the intricate details of the wooden handrails.

Entering his room, Jenson placed his now worn and weathered bag on the edge of the bed and sat down in a lonely slump. He missed the feeling he had at home – his connection to the land, being surrounded by forest, birds and crisp mountain air. Despite the luxuriousness of the hotel, it felt hollow in comparison to his place at Capertree.

The hotel restaurant was another thing altogether. Cloth napkins and oversized wine glasses sat atop a table that had more cutlery than Jenson knew what to do with. The wine glasses were filled at their arrival with a vintage that Hiram had apparently previously requested.

'I'm sure you will like this one,' Hiram said as the wine gurgled satisfyingly out of the full bottle. 'I was impressed with your cellar at the cabin. You clearly have an affinity for red wine and single-malt whisky.'

Jenson almost blushed with guilt at the comment after the work he had been doing. It all seemed so over the top and extraneous to him after living on the meagre portions of soup and stew following the disaster with Wolff's sled. He took a sip of the wine, feeling a wave of relaxation wash over him. The past forty-eight hours in particular had been hard to grasp. The emotion of survival was still raw and trying to suppress it while at the same time conjure a plan to sell their SK01 hypothesis was exhausting. Now, sitting here in a Swiss restaurant warmed by a crackling open fire and a glass of red wine, he finally felt he could take a moment to take stock and relax; even if just for this fleeting moment in time. The fire spat in protest as his eyes glazed over with the thought of forgetting everything for just a moment. Hiram then began to divulge the intricacies of his ideas to get their plan over the line. It seemed relatively simple when you boiled it down to the bare bones of it all.

As Hiram said in his own words, 'They really have no other choice but to follow our lead. There is no other research that has come close to revealing the cure for SK01. Plus, we have the most convincing case study in the world.' He pointed at his chest with a smile. 'Nobody can argue with that, can they?'

Jenson looked down at the folder in front of him that contained the summarised findings of their research. It was impressive, he knew that much, but he wasn't sure if it was enough at this stage. Hiram seemed more confident, which seemed to rub off on him.

'So you think you have them backed into a corner?' Jenson asked when the waiter arrived with their meal.

'It's more nuanced than that. We have two of the most prominent figures in SK01 mitigation presenting the argument.' Hiram gestured to the two of them. 'At this stage of the game, they would be brave to ignore what we're saying.'

The remainder of the meal was spent in deep discussion about the finer details of their results. Jenson gave first-hand explanations to the anecdotal evidence he had documented in the Congo and Greenland. The wine flowed and with that, their confidence seemed to as well.

Sleep was hard to come by for Jenson that night, despite the overwhelming fatigue, his aching body and blackened hands and feet. He studied the intricacies of the ceiling as his mind arrested any chance of a good night's rest before what might be the most critical meeting of his life. It came as a surprise when he was jolted awake in the early hours of the morning by a sudden thought transported through a dream. A soft grey glow crept from beneath the blinds to indicate the day had begun. He pulled the covers back and staggered to the bathroom where he ran the shower until it was piping hot before stepping in. The warm water soothed his joints and got his blood flowing. He ran his hands through his lengthening hair and beard to rid it of knots and relished in the feeling of being truly warm. He came out of the bathroom to find a black suit laid out on his bed, which had been made to impeccable precision. It was clearly the work of Abel, who remained a complete enigma to Jenson. He wondered if he'd somehow implanted a GPS tracker or vital signs indicator in his body. He seemed to know Jenson's every movement before he did.

The suit felt abnormal after weeks of dressing exclusively in gear designed for exploring sub-zero temperatures. The tie felt like a noose around his neck and tucking his shirt in just felt futile. He persisted with it anyway as his mind flashed forward to the delegates that he would be accompanied by in the coming hours. He had decided to keep his beard though, despite Abel trying to convince him otherwise. A knock at the door broke his thoughts about the peculiarity of human dress sense.

It was Abel. 'A car is ready for you downstairs when you're ready, Dr Ryder.'

Jenson nodded in recognition and finished the remnants of his morning coffee. The hot bittersweet liquid heightened his focus, like a weightlifter using sniffing salts before a big attempt. He glanced at himself in the mirror before going downstairs and couldn't believe the man that reflected back at him. He now appeared to be the academic version of Tarzan.

The meeting room was filled with the presence of a giant wooden table that was spotted by black office chairs carefully placed at even intervals around it. The room was benign, almost odourless and harboured a cleanliness that only the Swiss could master. The grey skies outside were muted by grey blinds leaving the soft yellow glow of the lights above to provide light to the room. Hiram was the only other person in there. He stood in the corner, gazing out of the only uncovered window to the cityscape of Geneva.

'Sleep well?' he asked.

Jenson shook his head as he took in the scene outside.

'Me too. Still, we must have confidence that this can get through. If we don't portray our conviction in the plan, how can we expect others to come on board?'

Jenson thought back to his suit, its discomfort plaguing him. He knew it was all part of the play though. Despite the fact billions of lives were now at stake, it remained pertinent to partake in society's dance to ensure he complied with its rules and norms. Perhaps that's why he kept the beard. To buck his path into normalcy. The door then opened and as Jenson and Hiram simultaneously looked around, a steady stream of people began to enter. They each took their designated seats and spoke softly so as not to disturb the baseline quiet of the room. The time had come. Hiram turned on the television screens at the front of the room and asked everyone to take their seats so they could begin.

'Thank you all for coming,' he began. 'As you are aware, we are in the midst of a worldwide crisis from the outbreak of SK01. Many of you have been tackling this plague with the thought that it is a communicable disease. However, I am here today, along with my colleague, to present our findings that indicate otherwise, along with a plan of action to mitigate SK01 altogether.'

Jenson's heart began to race as the stakes rose. He never said anything to Hiram about total elimination of SK01. The opening slide of Hiram's presentation flicked onto the screens at the front. Concerned faces looked in questioning interrogation, still trying to process the opening statement Hiram had hit them with. Whispers between chairs fluttered the room with immediate apprehension.

'We have multiple data sets from the areas of the globe where SK01 is most prevalent and from places where it is non-existent. Physiological readings, neural imaging and qualitative records indicate to us that SK01 is in fact a product of Anthropocene life rather than a disease transferred through viral or bacterial means.' Some additional graphs and tables appeared on the screen to back up his statement. 'Here we see the results of a patient with SK01 in its most advanced stage. There is distinct degradation of the amygdala, hippocampus and frontal lobe. This probably explains the reason why patients have such difficulty speaking and communicating. It is also the likely reason why such severe fatigue is taking place.'

Hiram left the room with a pause to allow for digestion of the information before them. He then clicked his laser pointer to the next slide. 'SK01 patients also display compromised functioning of the medulla oblongata. Ultimately, this could be the reason why SK01 produces human fatalities. This region of the brain has a major role in the control of respiration.'

Murmurs flickered through the hushed room until Hiram proceeded to his next slide.

'What appears to be our most profound research, however, is the observation that those who live in remote areas where there is limited access to technology and life is closer to that of our ancestral counterparts – these people are completely devoid of SK01. Not one single case has been reported in the regions we investigated. To better explain this phenomenon, I will invite Dr Jenson Ryder who carried out this field work to break it down.'

Jenson's heart was now in his mouth, which remained bone dry. The suit seemed to catch on every joint and protrusion as he levered his weary body from the office chair. Every pair of eyes in the room were fixated on him; this wild-looking and supposedly smart researcher. He cleared his throat and thanked Hiram for the introduction. Then, the words just seemed to flow. He began by speaking about his time in Tokyo, where he experienced the worst of SK01 and how this gave him the idea that a lack of synchronisation with the natural world could be a contributing factor to the disease.

'What we see in individuals studied in the remote areas of the Congo and Greenland is that their chronobiology remains aligned to what it has been for thousands of years. Their nutrition, their sleep and their social lives are relatively unchanged in that respect.' He focused his laser pointer on the screen to illustrate the effect of light exposure on the suprachiasmatic nucleus (SCN), 'which plays an integral role in sleep and overall wellbeing'. The SCN and cascade of neural and hormonal pathways were completely obliterated when looking at a patient with SK01.

'It is not only the SCN that is crucial in the pathophysiology of this disease,' Jenson tried to explain. 'Peripheral clocks that control the functioning of the various systems within the body appear to be misaligned to the SCN, which may be creating the onset of SK01. We're aware of adverse health effects resulting from a misalignment between the SCN and peripheral clocks; a phenomenon called circadian disruption.

'This is just the tip of the iceberg,' Jenson continued. 'We know that lack of exposure to natural light and natural environments is a contributor. So is the exposure to artificial light at night. There are also other clear elements of "civilised life" that are having an effect, such as the nutritional quality, time spent engaged with technological devices and the level of physical activity undertaken on a daily basis. We have cross-matched hundreds of data points that give a causation effect to this hypothesis and these are just the ones we know about. There are bound to be others; known unknowns and unknown unknowns.'

By now, the room was stunned into complete silence. Blank faces were left reeling at the proposal that life itself was the cause for such a vicious and wide-spread disease. Jenson took a breath and assessed the situation. He could sense the tension, the anticipation and the confusion. There was a heaviness to it that he hadn't felt since returning from Greenland. Finally, a member from the United Nations spoke up.

'You're telling us that the very way we live our lives is the reason for this pandemic?'

Jenson nodded in agreeance, nervous that any further dialogue from his mouth would set the room alight with controversy. The man who asked the question locked eyes with Jenson for what seemed like an eternity. He had a moustache and black-framed glasses that reflected the screen at the front of the room and like everyone else, he wore a black suit and tie with a white shirt.

'So what do you propose, Dr Ryder?' he eventually said.

Jenson had been so consumed with presenting a convincing case that SK01 wasn't a communicable disease that he had almost neglected to think about the mitigation strategies he had discussed with Hiram. The focus seemed to be on the pitch rather than the solution. He swept the loose strands of sandy blonde hair from his eyes and smiled gently.

'This is where it gets more complex.'

'And the disruption of the human suprachiasmatic nucleus is simple?' someone sarcastically noted before he could continue.

He was thankful for the comment as the tension in the air dissipated and allowed Jenson some leniency that had been all but sucked dry by the heaviness of the subject.

'Our strategies at this stage a crude, at best,' he began. 'From a case study, we know that the symptoms can be reduced quickly if the patient undergoes a restorative period. That is, they remove themselves from their current environment in order to "reset" their SCN and peripheral clocks. So, placing a limit on artificial light, technology and processed food, for example. Immersion in the natural environment also appears to be a key component in the recovery phase.' Jenson glanced over at Hiram, who was seated in the corner with a wry smile on his face.

'So your strategy is to return to the Stone Age, Dr Ryder?' the man with black-framed glasses asked.

'It may look like that from the outside, but no. It is simply to live a more balanced life that is integrated into the natural environment. Cultures all over the world have this running through their heritage. The Japanese have long spoken about *shinrin-yoku*, essentially immersion in the forest for the benefit of health. Scandinavians have *friluftsliv*, which teaches people to embrace nature for spiritual and physical wellbeing. This is not a foreign concept and while the separation away from the natural environment has been increasing for some time, it is only in the past decade or so that it has accelerated at such a rate. Therefore, we see the worst-hit areas are big cities: Tokyo, Paris, Rome, New York. You've all seen the data. There is a reason for this. At first, it made sense to assume this was because of close living proximities leading to the spread of a virus, but we are now confident that this hypothesis is incorrect. Instead, we believe it's because these are the places where humans are most divorced from nature, where circadian disruption is at its most prominent and where abnormal living environments are commonplace.'

Further silence followed as people shifted uncomfortably in their seats. Hiram stood up and began to walk over to Jenson.

'What we are proposing today is not a long-term solution. It is simply to get SK01 under wraps and allow us to develop a more sustainable strategy.'

A flurry of objection erupted as the reality of what was required sank in. Arguments were being spat across every direction of the table in a smattering of different languages. Eventually, one person rose above the cacophony. It was the same protagonist who had been heckling Jenson through his entire presentation.

'There is no way an entire country can ask this of its people. Our economy will crash, our way of life will disintegrate.'

The rest of the room joined the chorus of disapproval and before long, the room was in a messy cacophony of violent spats once again. Jenson stood resolute at the front of the room, observing the disdain written across the faces of everyone else.

'Look at what you have now.' Nobody heard him over the noise of argumentative conversation. 'Look at what you have now!'

The room fell silent and all eyes fell upon Jenson standing at the front. He placed both hands upon the table in front of him and stared at the man who had created the catalyst for the nonsense that ensued. 'You say this plan will kill your country, your economy, your way of life. Look at what SK01 has done to it already. It will only worsen if you ignore it. We may need to take a few steps back to make a giant leap forward. That is often the way in circumstances where we're on the precipice. We just need your consideration and your trust so we can finally get on top of this monster. So, if you want to destroy your country, go ahead, take our advice and throw it in the trash.'

Jenson could see his words echo through the minds of every other person sitting around the table. Their eyes were now fixated on the grains of wood in front of them or at their twiddling thumbs in their laps. Hiram's prediction that they had nothing else to fall back on was clearly a factor after all. They were all at a loss at what to do. That had been clear for a long time. The sheer enormity of Jenson's left-of-field proposal had caught them off guard though. They had been shocked back into reality, like an electrical current surging the grid. Something had to give. Slowly, the life came back to the room and Jenson sensed it was now time to get to the crux of the pitch: the solution.

'I assume you all want to get on top of SK01 and eventually get rid of it altogether?' Jenson began.

There was little response from anyone as they continued to stare blankly at each other

'As Hiram mentioned earlier, this plan is simply a temporary measure and we will need to assess it as it's rolled out. We'll probably need to tweak things along the way and likely get some things wrong. You must understand that we are not experts in this yet. We still have much to understand and like everyone here today, we have been impacted by SK01. Whether that be from a loved one, a colleague or simply the country you represent, this has been something that has touched us all.'

Hiram was still standing off to the side while Jenson spoke, observing the gradual shifts in demeanour from those in the room. Everyone seemed to be listening intently. Perhaps the realisation that they were all in this together was a comfort to them. Shared trauma so often brought people together in the long term.

Jenson laid out the recommendations he had developed with Hiram, Nya and Emerson off the back of their research. They were crude and somewhat vague, but it was essential that the information be disseminated as soon as possible.

'Exposure to the natural environment is critical. Whether that be a garden in the middle of a city, a remote stretch of beach or a mountain range that you have access to. Exposure needs to be frequent and sustained for at least a fortnight in those who are showing signs of SK01.' Jenson was encouraged by the sudden engagement everyone seemed to be showing. Keyboards were being tapped away on as he spoke while others furiously wrote notes by hand.

He continued, buoyed by their commitment. 'Rest assured, we will provide you all with a copy of our recommendations at the conclusion of this meeting.' He paused and then continued to describe the remaining changes listed on the document in front of him. 'Entrainment of natural circadian rhythm through the appropriate stimulation of the SCN is also crucial. Exposure to natural light during the day and limits to artificial light at night are critical in this regard. We also recommend the restriction of exposure to wireless internet sources in those who are acutely affected. Furthermore, the use of personal electronic devices should be all but stopped in those worse affected, while others should drastically reduce their exposure.'

This seemed to raise the eyebrows of some around the table as their thoughts drifted to how that would be managed.

'We also recommend the restriction of artificial and processed food sources such as preservatives, colours, additives, et cetera. A diet that is primarily made up of "real food" is what we are advocating at this point. Appropriate chrononutrition practices should also be implemented to ensure alignment of peripheral clocks and the SCN.'

Jenson continued for well over an hour, describing in detail the practices that their research had highlighted as the key drivers of resistance and recovery from SK01. After he had finished talking, there seemed to be a renewed level of optimism in the room. Jenson looked over at Hiram who had taken his seat in the corner. He simply nodded and smiled. The glint in his eye was enough to return Jenson's heart rate to normal again. Eventually, everyone left the room and it was just the two of them again. They sat silent and alone, staring out the same corner window they convened at before it began. The grey skies of Geneva dampened the footpaths below and mist shrouded the surrounding mountains that enveloped the lake. They were almost in a trance after pulling off what Nya had said was 'mission impossible'.

'What now?' Jenson finally said, his eyes still transfixed on Lake Geneva, with its endless fountain spurting water into the air.

Hiram paused and took his gaze away from the picturesque scenes out the window. 'We follow our own advice.'

CHAPTER 38

Sasha's TV cut suddenly to a breaking news segment that caught her attention. She had been confined to the house again for the past few days with the same symptoms she experienced a few months earlier. The pain in her mind had not been as intense and she was able to talk properly most of the time. However, the lethargy and confusion remained a constant companion in the background of her mind.

'*This is a service announcement from the World Health Organisation in association with national and international security agencies,*' the newsreader began. '*You will all be aware of the recent epidemic of SK01 that has swept the world. We can present to you tonight that health and security agencies around the world have made progress on the mitigation of SK01 and issued the following statement:*

"SK01 has been identified as a product of lifestyle and not an infectious bacteria or virus. This means the disease cannot be spread from person to person but is rather a product of our environment."'

The statement continued for a couple of minutes, outlining the recommendations that people undertake to mitigate the effects of or reduce their vulnerability to SK01. The vision cut back to the newsreader and then to a live cross of a press conference in Geneva, Switzerland. Sasha sat stunned, looking at the television set that illuminated the darkened living room as she saw her ex-husband standing behind the lectern informing the world of how to manage SK01. She had to squint at the TV to make sure it was actually Jenson. She had never seen him with such an unwieldy beard and the suit just didn't seem right on him.

She placed her hand up to her mouth and let out a small sob. For all the time they had spent together as a married couple, she had been so reluctant to partake in any of his interests, as most of them involved isolation in the depths of the wilderness. Things started to come together in her mind as she pieced together the confusing aspects of the passing months. She had desperately tried to contact Jenson over that time but could not get through and now understood why.

Over the coming days, Sasha implemented the recommendations set out by the WHO. She turned the WiFi router off, stopped using personal electronic devices, ensured she got adequate sunlight during the day and went for a walk around the local lake each day, often sitting by the water's edge for an hour so afterwards to just stop and listen to the lapping of the water and the occasional squawk of a swan. Workplaces across the country allowed their employees to take time away from their jobs to ensure the recommendations were being implemented properly. Many predicted that the economy would come to a grinding halt and the world would cave in. However, apart from some civil unrest in pockets of certain countries, there was little report of ill effects from the overhaul. News reports about the ridiculous requests set by the WHO slowly declined and were eventually replaced by stories of renewal and hope. Expert after expert had been interviewed on every television show across the world. Some were supportive but most grilled the recommendations. Once the results started to speak for themselves, the naysayers quickly faded into the background and were left to fight for their survival in the cold isolation of society.

Sasha stuck to her routine and found her sleep improved. With that, her energy levels and neurological function seemed to bounce back as well. In two weeks, she had little to no symptoms at all after battling with the mystery illness for months prior. She went next door to check on her neighbour, Michelle. The last time she had seen her she was convinced she was dead. There was barely a pulse and her skin had turned a shade of grey. She knocked on the door and to her amazement, she answered.

Sasha stood in stunned silence for a moment before she spoke.

'Michelle, you're… you're okay.'

She smiled. 'Thanks to your ex-husband.'

Sasha blushed and felt a confusing mix of pride and guilt at the comment.

'Come in. We have a lot to catch up on.'

CHAPTER 39

A month had passed since that all-important meeting. Jenson and Hiram stepped onto the plane as the jet engines started to turn. Jenson had been on the road for over four months in some of the most hostile and arduous of conditions. The past month had been far more comfortable as they took up quarters in Geneva to assist with the SK01 mitigation roll-out. Since being in Switzerland, he had regained his strength and mental fortitude, which had been sapped by the icy cold and starvation of the Greenland expedition. Despite that, he had unwillingly inherited the title of SK01 expert and face of the management campaign.

As an introverted and humble man, it sat uncomfortably with him but Hiram had encouraged him to embrace it and lean into the responsibility. There was no doubt he would forever be a changed person after the events since taking that fateful phone call from Hiram all those months ago. Duties beyond the safe confines of Switzerland now called, though. He was required to travel on a speaking tour to a range of rebel countries, which had experienced a backlash to the recommendations. The primary purpose was to provide assurances to governments and citizens on their proposals. It was hoped the presence of Jenson, as the face of SK01, would alleviate concerns.

As the plane banked to the south, the Swiss Alps glowed softly in the evening light, The Matterhorn was just visible in the distance with its iconic peak jutting out from the clouds that shrouded the base. Jenson thought of his house back on the banks of the Capertree River, with smoke idly climbing from the chimney in the cold morning air as whip bird calls echoed out from down the valley. He missed his isolation and autonomy but reminded himself that what he was doing was for the greater good. He would have plenty of time to live that life after all this was done, he thought, as he peered out the small windows of the jet. There was nothing quite like the Swiss Alps from the air.

Since the meeting, they had taken on extreme criticism and drawback from governments on almost every continent. Despite sending their health and security delegates off from the meeting with a positive frame of mind and an eagerness to persuade their nations to implement change, the initial operation of the recommendations had been met with stone-cold resistance. The typical responses were shouted down the end of the telephone and videoconference calls day after day with abuse that often bordered the line on personal attack. Wave after wave of requests came through for meetings with Hiram and Jenson to discuss the 'utter ridiculousness' of the proposal, as one country's President had described it. The security and health delegates that had met that first day had come back to them in complete despair at times. One such member had been fired by their government for proposing the plan. It was left to Jenson to console them, battered and despondent on the other end of an international call. Their days were filled with these types of exchanges in the first fortnight before the tide slowly began to turn.

Change started to become noticeable in the countries that diligently implemented the recommendations. Scandinavia showed rapid improvement after imposing strict restrictions on internet usage, particularly on social media channels. In a matter of days, Norway reported the remission of SK01 patients. The positive news had a snowball effect through Europe and eventually in Asia and across to North and South America. Stepping onto the plane a month later, Jenson and Hiram were confident every populated continent on the planet had seen some improvement in their management of SK01. Nya and Emerson had created a model that provided ongoing updates to the number of cases around the world. Visual representation slowly saw the image turn from red, indicating high rates of SK01 to yellow, orange, blue and finally green in some areas where the disease had been overturned. News reports regularly used the visual to provide updates on the crisis and the supposed 'miracle cure inspired by our ancient ancestors' as one reporter had framed it. Jenson cringed at the statement when he first heard it but it seemed to catch on and gave the public something to grab onto in order to materialise the treatment. He remembered the bemusement surrounding the SCN when he first introduced it in the meeting to people who were highly intelligent. It was unlikely then, he thought, that the everyday man or woman would be able to grapple at the neurobiology of what was occurring. Whatever promoted adherence had to be beneficial, he supposed.

While the results were largely positive, there had been some upheaval in pockets of the world. Eastern Europe and northern Africa had broken out into civil unrest. Street riots, violence and loitering had become an increasing problem. It had started with a faction of non-believers who protested against the proposed recommendations. They had gained significant support to rally against their governments, despite most members of the group having loved ones affected by SK01. Jenson found the situation frustrating but it was now his job to spend time in these nations and speak about the mitigation measures on the ground. Hiram would accompany him in the initial phase and then return to HQ once the schedule was up and running. Nya and Emerson continued to be the drivers of CINS but required support that only their leader could provide. Abel was designated to stay on with Jenson for logistical support.

The pilot came over the intercom to give an update on weather conditions and travel time. It was a little strange when it was basically just Hiram, Jenson and Abel he was providing the update to. Jenson realised he had no idea who the pilot was. The man had been escorting them around the world these past few months and along with the flight staff, had always been vigilant and attentive to their needs when they were in the air. Their timing seemed to be always impeccable as well. Never had they had a delay in their arrival or departure. They had obviously been extensively screened and cleared by CINS to operate in this environment. He wondered if they had been in Switzerland this past month waiting for the day they were required or whether they had been called out to other jobs around the globe. Jenson's mind was brought back to the present as one of the staff members provided him with a drink and some snacks. They had become so well acquainted that they even knew what he liked to eat and drink.

Their first stop was in Istanbul, Turkey. From there, they would travel up Eastern Europe, encompassing Sofia, Bulgaria and Bucharest in Romania. After the European tour had finished, they would then fly south to Africa to meet with the governments of Libya, Tunisia and Algeria. These remained the most reluctant nations to implement change and it was critical to get them under control. Nobody knew what the long-term effects of SK01 were. The first reported case had been less than nine months ago and most of the severe cases were now being alleviated through WHO management strategies. There was still the fear of the unknown in those who had not gone into remission though. Was there a time at which the condition took hold so deeply that it never let go? Could patients be forever trapped inside an aching and lifeless mind and a body that was screaming to be released from its shackles?

CHAPTER 40

Stepping onto Turkish soil for the first time, Jenson was met with the salty air that was expected for a city that was cradled between two bodies of ocean; the Sea of Marmara and the Black Sea. Seagulls squawked overhead as they crossed the tarmac into yet another airport. The most agitating thing for Jenson since Greenland had been the lack of opportunity to explore his surroundings. He had been so consumed by the task at hand that he hadn't had the chance to properly see Switzerland and all the beauty it contained. There had been a few days here and there he had managed to sneak in a day hike around the mountains near Geneva but nothing compared to what he would've liked. The dramatic mountains seemed to peer down on him, sleeved in ice, waiting for him to explore their nuances. He hoped the next few countries would not be just airports, hotels and strangers. He had to remind himself to practice what he was preaching. Time in nature was more critical to Jenson than most other aspects of life. His task now was to pass that enthusiasm onto others.

Their arrival at the hotel coincided with a beautiful sunset over the city. The silhouette of mosques contrasted against the pastel blue evening sky. Jenson's room opened right up to the edge of the Bosporus, the narrow stretch of water that connected the two seas on either side of the city. The streets were alive with people as they funnelled their way through the narrow streets below. Foreign voices echoed along with the aroma of spices and cooked meat. The evening prayer call blasted out from loudspeakers, catching Jenson off guard. He leaned on the balcony and soaked in the warm evening air that was laced with salt and spice and wondered why there had been such resistance in a place that had such a strong geographical connection to the ocean.

Hiram joined Jenson out on the balcony and offered him a beer. The two of them simultaneously took a swig and continued to absorb the foreign atmosphere of a new city.

'We meet with the security agency tomorrow,' Hiram said, breaking the silence.

Jenson met the comment with a nod and another sip of beer. 'Are we bound to fail or do they have their ears open?'

'Depends who you talk to, as usual. We'll need our best debating skills on hand though.'

The comment provided little solace to Jenson's already biased thoughts on being on a speaking tour to spruik the SK01 mitigation proposal. The politics of it all was what was most frustrating. Like many things, even if the evidence was clear, bureaucracy could still manage to get in the way.

Jenson tossed and turned in the early hours of the morning. It had been a restless night, to say the least. The constant mulling and weight of expectation were beginning to take their toll on his mind. The antique clock hanging on the wall across the room indicated it was 4.30 a.m. There was little hope in getting back to sleep so he climbed out of bed and put his running gear on. A faint glow of light had appeared across the strait; the ocean soaked it in and reflected an oily liquidity as it gently flapped like a sheet in a summer breeze. Jenson ran softly along the cobbled streets, past the usually bustling tourist attractions of Blue Mosque and Hagia Sophia. There was an eeriness about them at this time of day. *If their walls could talk*, Jenson thought as he trotted past.

Returning to the hotel, an increasing number of people were making their way onto the streets to begin their day. Jenson climbed into the shower and began the arduous process of putting his suit and tie on for their meeting with the Turkish government security and health agencies. If Hiram's anecdotal evidence had indicated anything, it would not be all smooth sailing once they entered that room.

'They have strong opinions, let's just say that much,' he had said when they were discussing their approach on the plane.

A vocal crowd could be heard outside Jenson's window and it seemed to be growing louder. He adjusted the knot of his tie and peered out the window to see what the commotion was about. As his head jutted out over the balcony to gain a better view, he could see a mass of people swarming through the streets below. They were congregating around the embassy where their meeting was scheduled, not far from the hotel. Angry chants and placards were being hoisted in the air in protest. It was then he heard a knock at the door. Opening it, he found Abel in a rare state of fluster.

'Dr Ryder, we must leave at once. Are you ready?'

Jenson grabbed his laptop from the bedside table and raced down the stairs in pursuit of Abel.

'Do you want to tell me what the fuck is going on out there before we walk right into it?' he shouted down the stairwell as his feet tried desperately to keep up with the descent.

'It appears the SK01 resistance army have got wind of your arrival in Istanbul.'

'Who leaked the intel? What do they want with us?'

'I have no idea at this stage, Dr Ryder. Now hurry up!'

The streets were clear as they scurried outside and met Hiram near the hotel lobby. The protesting chants were gaining volume, echoing through the cobbled streets. Jenson felt them closing in with each racing heartbeat. Armed guards appeared out of nowhere as they turned a bend. The AK47s hanging casually off their shoulders halted Jenson in his tracks, thinking they had been cajoled into a corner. A few seconds passed before one of the guards indicated to follow him through the armoured gates of the consulate and to safety. In all the past expeditions and months of work with CINS, this was the first time an armoured guard had been required. The snap of the lock on wrought iron gates provided some degree of assurance as they gathered themselves before walking into the building.

Jenson turned to see the protesters rounding the bend and closing in on the gates they had just been escorted through. Angry faces blended into an angry crowd as they drew closer and ever louder.

'Jenson.' Hiram gestured for him to come inside as his eyes lay transfixed on the shouting mob before them.

'Have the chopper on standby if this thing goes south, okay?' Hiram said to Abel, as they made their way past reception.

The meeting room smelled of cigarette smoke and coffee as the door was opened for them. Three men who sat at the table were conversing in Turkish. They stood up to greet Hiram and Jenson as they entered.

'Please, sit down,' one man said, his thick black moustache adding a layer to his accent. 'Can I get you anything? Coffee? Tea? Whisky?'

'I don't anticipate we'll be here long, so let's get this underway, shall we?' Hiram responded.

Mr Yousef Aslan was the key in all this mess. He sat across from them with his arms crossed and a vague expression of disinterest smeared across his tanned face. A dark five o'clock shadow concealed the acne scars across his cheeks and a thin band of smoke rose from the cigarette that hung loosely from his fingers.

'Please excuse the fiasco outside, gentlemen. I assure you their voices are louder than their powers around here.' Mr Aslan took a long and deep drag from his cigarette before exhaling the smoke across at Jenson. 'Today is about coming to a resolution to put these people back in their box, yes?'

Jenson looked suspiciously across at Hiram before answering. 'Mr Aslan, may I ask how the findings from the WHO report on SK01 were disseminated to the general public through Turkey, and particularly Istanbul?'

A long silence ensued as Yousef took a deep drag of his cigarette and relaxed back into his wooden chair. It creaked with tension as he slumped back and then finally answered.

'Dr Ryder, we followed WHO protocol in distributing your recommendations. But the people of Turkey are sceptical of them. They are naturally sceptical of the larger nations such as the United States and those in the European Union. It is very convenient of them to tell the rest of the world what to do when they have the resources to do it.' He paused again for a long time, this time choosing to let his cigarette burn but never ash. 'Take a look at the nations who are rebelling against this cause. They are all in the lower spectrum of world GDP. They cannot afford to simply "switch off" and "connect to our ancestral roots" as you have previously said.'

The protesting shouts and chants were growing louder as the discussion unfolded. Yousef seemed more interested in passing the blame back to Hiram and his team, mostly Jenson, for the way in which the recommendations were passed down through the WHO. Before they were able to retort, the adjacent window to where they were seated was smashed by a Molotov cocktail, which then rolled across the table in front of them.

'Get the hell out of here!' Yousef shouted as his soft, round body sprinted towards the door. It had been some time since he had moved that quickly.

Jenson, Hiram and the other Turkish delegates followed and slammed the door before the explosion obliterated the room. Hiram was immediately on the phone to Abel.

'What's the status of the chopper?' he yelled down the speaker.

Anxious moments passed while Jenson waited for Abel's response and for Hiram to relay it.

'Head to the roof. We've got exfil coming in five minutes.'

They raced up the stairs, leaving Yousef and his colleagues to fend for themselves. It was their mess, Hiram reasoned with himself, his legs burning from the lactate accumulation after countless flights of stairs. They burst open the solid steel hatch and entered the rooftop, squinting in the early morning sun that reflected from the concrete. They could hear the protesters below, smashing glass and clambering the iron gates at the front. It would only be a matter of time before they scaled the fences and entered the premises. Just as the thought of bunkering on the roof for an extended Jenson's mind, the familiar clap of helicopter rotors echoed from the horizon. A winch line was dropped from the cockpit to get the men up into the aircraft and whisked away to safety.

Hiram was heaved up first and the winch line returned to retrieve Abel and finally Jenson. Jenson could hear the rattling gates being burst open and the shouts ascending the stairs where rioters were on a singular mission for their blood. It was his own selflessness that left him stranded on the exposed concrete rooftop, waiting for the line to descend from the helicopter. He had demanded that Hiram go up first, screaming the instruction above the roar of the helicopter blades. He clipped into the harness and expected to be lifted from up to the cockpit. Instead, the helicopter just rose and banked away, leaving him dangling like bait on the end of a fishing line. He held the line tight as they picked up speed and effortlessly glided just above the cityscape.

As they ascended from the grips of Istanbul's chaos, the true scope of the upheaval dawned upon them. Spot fires could be seen dotted across the inner-city centre with rioters swarming towards the gates of the embassy. Word had clearly spread of their meeting and the masses had taken it upon themselves to take matters into their own hands. The helicopter banked away to the west and headed away from the rising sun and across the sea of Marmara and into the arms of the Aegean, hopefully to safety. The smell of the salt air suddenly hit as they fled the mainland, leaving behind the smoke, sweat and spice of the city. Jenson's white-knuckle grip on the winch line eased slightly as the realisation they had escaped a witch-hunt became reality. He had no idea where they were headed but he was glad they were escaping the dangers of what he had just experienced. The scale of disorganisation and disagreement as a result of the WHO recommendations was only just starting the rear its head. The thought of continuing a tour of similarly affected countries suddenly seemed like a terrible idea. He put the thought out of his mind and gazed out across the sea and tried to appreciate the fact he was getting the experience of a lifetime by dangling out of a helicopter in the middle of the Mediterranean.

He sighted land after about forty-five minutes and realised immediately where they were heading. The unmistakable coastline of Athens presented itself in the morning light, its white cliff tops illuminated softly against the sparkling ocean. Ancient landmarks made themselves known as they traversed the coastline that was dotted with block-like houses painted impeccably with the purist of white paint. After doing some reconnaissance of the area, the pilot found an appropriate place to land. It required Jenson to unclip from the winch line first while they hovered above. His legs dangled precariously above a building top in the city centre before he was confident enough to release his carabiner and drop a short distance onto the concrete below. His black dress shoes provided less than ideal shock absorption from the fall and his suit restricted his movement as he tried in vain to roll upon impact. Clambering to his feet, he looked up to the helicopter and gave the all-clear signal for them to land.

'Sorry about the transportation,' Hiram said as they reunited after landing. 'There was no more room left in the cabin. Plus, you did insist we all go up before you.'

Jenson smiled at the comment, happy the ordeal was now over. 'I think I can forgive you. After all, the view wasn't bad from my vantage.'

There was a pause as they waited for the helicopter to take off.

'So, where are we?' he asked of Hiram as they descended the stairs of the unknown building.

'Greek consulate,' he casually responded, barely breaking stride.

'And they know we're coming, of course?'

'Of course.'

The sheer nonchalance of the man amused Jenson more than anything.

'And where to from here?' he followed up, unwilling to let the topic go.

He was cut short as they exited through a stairwell door and into the main building. The office staff whose area they suddenly emerged into simultaneously stopped and turned. The entire room stared at Jenson and Hiram who had burst through the door in their suits, dishevelled from being transported across the Aegean in a helicopter after escaping a civil riot. Neither of them knew any Greek so they awkwardly waved to their new audience and proceeded out the exit and down to the level where they hoped someone would know who they were.

'Do you even know where we are?' Jenson continued to probe.

'We're supposed to be at our government consulate office, but I have no idea who our Greek representative is at the moment.'

The tether that was holding Hiram's fortitude in place was growing ever weaker as they scaled the stairs in hope that they would find someone or something that looked familiar. It wasn't until they reached the ground floor and spoke to reception that they were advised they were in the wrong building. The office they were after was, in fact, directly across the street. Hiram's head hung defeatedly as he turned away from the receptionist and proceeded out the door and across the street. Jenson followed, thanking the woman behind the desk and apologising for Hiram's lack of enthusiasm for her assistance.

'It's been a rough day,' he explained as he said goodbye.

Eventually, they found their Greek counterpart in the office across the street and travel plans were organised to get Hiram, Abel and Jenson back to CINS Headquarters. In a moment of utter exhaustion and defeat, Hiram decided it was better to leave the tour of rebel nations until safety could be guaranteed. For now, it was time to focus on continuing their efforts and concentrating on the positives. The majority of the world's nations had implemented some portion of the WHO recommendations and were seeing positive results. Circadian biologists, ancestral geneticists and various other human health experts were recruited by governments across the globe to carry out plans. The movement had been dubbed 'Operation Ancestor' as news corporations grabbed at every opportunity to embellish the so-called cure for SK01. Hiram also concluded that there was more they could do from HQ than flying across the globe chasing the tails of those who failed to see the bigger picture. Emerson and Nya had been continuing to collect data, which could help facilitate the next stage of their plan in mitigating SK01 altogether.

For Jenson, it was a relief to know that he wouldn't have a repeat of what had happened today. He was still wrapping his head around the situation and the events of the day. Sitting at the hotel bar with a glass of whisky, his shoulders slouched over the wooden bench and looking deep into the glass before him, he reflected on the escape they had made. Flashbacks of the anxious moments he spent on the exposed rooftop were seared into his mind. It was difficult to comprehend that someone was after his head when all he set out to do was help them. He took another swig from his glass. Hiram sat next to him, barely saying a word. Jenson was wary not to hassle him too much but it was clear that the ugly symptoms of SK01 had returned. They had had a hectic schedule of late, the opposite advice to what they had been prescribing for those recuperating from the condition. Nya had warned the both of them to be on the lookout for symptoms and ensure adequate sleep and sunlight exposure were adhered to. Considering the time zones they'd crossed of late, he was sure their circadian rhythms were so far out of synch it would take weeks for them to get back to something that rendered normality.

'You should get some rest,' Jenson finally said after taking a sip.

There was a long pause before Hiram looked across the bar and nodded.

'I don't know about you, but I'm spent.' He rubbed the top of his bald head and then sunk his face deep into his palms. 'We've got transport arranged for 0900 tomorrow. A car will be waiting out the front of the hotel lobby. Make sure you're there, sharp.' He drained the rest of his glass and patted Jenson on the shoulder as he walked past on his way to the elevators.

'0900. See you then.'

At least he was still speaking, Jenson thought to himself as he ordered another drink from the bartender. He told himself this would be the last one.

CHAPTER 41

Hiram woke with a start and had no idea where he was. The sounds of smashing glass and Molotov cocktails reverberated through his mind as he sat up to take stock of where he was. Another hotel room, he suddenly realised, as his heart rate began to return to resting levels. He rubbed the sleep from his eyes and saw the time was 5.06 a.m. The illuminated numbers on the clock dial faded in and out of focus as he looked vaguely around at the room. He wouldn't be going back to sleep again, so he got up and took a cold shower in an effort to jolt his body awake.

The water trickled down his neck and shoulders, causing goosebumps to sprout up over his arms and torso. It was then he felt a strange pulsating feeling through his body, almost like a mild current of electricity. He steadied himself with a hand on the shower wall and looked down at his feet. The water trickled down the drain with an echo as he tried to restore his senses. It didn't seem to work and in a matter of moments, he was in excruciating agony and doubled over on the shower floor. The water continued to run and now felt like piercing bolts of electricity stabbing into his skin. He tried to cry out in pain, but nothing seemed to compute.

What the hell was in that whisky? he thought to himself as staggered to his feet to turn the water off. It took every ounce of energy to get his back rested up against the wall and reach for the faucets. He tilted his head back against the tiles to rest, out of breath and struggling to comprehend what was happening to him. Just as quickly as the pain had seared its way through every neuron in his body, he realised what was happening to him. Once again, he tried to scream out, this time in frustration, anger and self-pity but nothing came out. He couldn't move, he couldn't speak, and he was in an astonishing degree of pain lying naked in a hotel shower.

CHAPTER 42

A black van pulled into the hotel lobby parking and a suited man with dark sunglasses exited the driver door. Jenson took a few confident strides up to him and shook his hand before loading his belongings and stepping in. It was 8.55 a.m. and he was eager to get on the road to the airport, where their air transportation was waiting to jet back to Headquarters. He'd had enough of the politics surrounding SK01 and was longing to get back to his day-to-day operations on the ground. As far as he was concerned, they had done their due diligence and the baton had been passed to the WHO and the authorities of each respective nation. In just a couple of months, they had practically put a halt to new cases of SK01 and the recuperation efforts on those affected by the condition were now underway as well. All that remained was to monitor the progress of the condition and ensure it was kept under wraps. Ultimately, that was Hiram's job anyway. Jenson had spent the past three months or more on the road solving the problem. Maybe this was the moment he could return home and pursue something resembling normality again. The issue of rebel nations unwilling to cooperate with the recommendations and subsequently continuing to suffer was a case of simple ineptitude in his opinion now. The patience and empathy he'd first displayed when hearing of their troubles had now evaporated. A direct threat to life could do that. He looked down impatiently at his wristwatch to check the time; it was almost 9.00 a.m. It was unlike Hiram to cut the time so close to schedule and he had been specific before leaving the bar last night that he was to be there on time.

'Are we good to go?' the driver asked as he got into the van.

'Still waiting on one.'

'We don't want to cut it fine. You know what airports are like.'

Jenson nodded at the driver. 'Give me five minutes. I'll head up to his room to check what's going on.'

'Five minutes. No more. We're under strict instructions.'

Knocking on the door, Jenson received nothing but silence in return. He tried to peer through the peephole in the door but couldn't make out anything substantial.

'Hiram!' he shouted. 'Hiram!' He knocked violently on the wooden door again but to no avail.

A cleaner came around the corner of the corridor as he started pacing back and forth outside the room.

'Excuse me, ma'am,' he said, trying to calm himself down so as not to frighten her away. 'Do you speak English?'

She shook her head in response but this seemed like the best option at present, so he persisted in trying to talk to her anyway.

'Ahh, my friend'—he gestured to the door—'he is supposed to be in this room. Can you check if he is inside?'

She shook her head in response once again and began walking past the room. Jenson grabbed her arm – harder than he would've liked, but his anxiousness was getting the better of him.

'Please,' he said softly. 'My friend was supposed to be meeting me this morning. I need to know if he's in this room.'

He gestured once more to the door, indicating that he wanted her to open it. The isolation of the corridor didn't help Jenson's wish to appease her but she finally relented.

'Quickly,' she said in a thick Greek accent.

The door creaked slowly open to reveal nothing but an unmade bed and some clothing hanging off a chair in the corner. The curtains remained drawn, blocking the harsh morning sun from heating the room. It left a dankness in the air as a result. There appeared no sign of Hiram as Jenson perused the room, stepping carefully around the perimeter.

'Not here,' the cleaner said, breaking the silence. 'Time to go.'

Jenson held his index finger in the air, indicating he needed one more minute. There was something not quite right about the situation. It was as if Hiram had just walked out with nothing but the clothes on his back and never come back.

A triangle of light caught his eye around the corner of the room so he followed it. The bathroom door was ajar, with the light filtering out from its opening. Stepping towards it, he slowly opened the door to see Hiram curled at the base of the shower, shivering and naked. Words seemed to be lost to Jenson in that moment.

'Hiram?' he finally managed to say. 'Hiram, what's going on?'

There was nothing in response but a pained look on his face.

Jenson crouched down outside the shower and looked at Hiram. He knew that look, he suddenly thought. He knew exactly what it represented and had seen it on the faces of dozens of people in the past months. The feeling of wanting to speak, wanting to move, but not being able to. It was the haunting, trapped look of someone with SK01.

'Fuck,' he muttered under his breath as he stood up.

There was no way he was letting him stay another day in this region; they had to get back to HQ as quickly as possible, even if that meant transporting an incapacitated Hiram at the same time. The risk was too great; yesterday's events had clearly indicated that much. He turned around to see the cleaner standing in the doorway with a mortified look strewn across her face. It didn't look good. A naked man cradled in the corner of a hotel shower while the man who requested access to the room paced anxiously in pursuit of an answer to the situation. Jenson could sense her unease and see the thoughts racing through her mind.

'The towel,' he said, pointing to the stereotypical white towel hanging on the railing behind her. 'Pass me the towel. Please.'

Still confused, she did as Jenson requested before turning around and heading out the door and straight to the elevators.

'Fuck,' he said, louder this time. 'C'mon, let's get some clothes on you and get the hell out of here.'

Hiram was not a short man, making it difficult for him to wrap the towel around him and heave his lifeless body over to the bed where he struggled to dress him. He grabbed the clothes that were lying around the room from the night before and hurriedly found himself dressing a fully-grown man. Yet another situation he would've laughed at had someone told him he'd be doing this just a few short months prior. He was cognisant of the fact that the cleaner was probably down at reception by now telling the hotel staff that a man was lying in a shower, practically lifeless, with Jenson the prime suspect.

Sweat started to bead on his forehead as he hoisted Hiram over his shoulder like a sack of flour. It was ungracious and brutal to treat a sick man this way but he knew there was no other option. He was about to head to the elevator but realised it led straight into the arms of the waiting hotel staff. Instead, he kicked the door to the fire escape stairs and began the lengthy descent. By the time he reached the bottom floor, his knees were shaking from the load. His five minutes was nearly up and there was no way he was letting this situation escalate any further. Sweat streamed down his face and into his whiskers as he picked up the pace around to the parking lobby. The black van remained, idling and ready to go with the driver leaning on the door.

'Give me a hand, will you?' Jenson said as he approached the van.

The driver, clearly stunned, took a few moments to realise it was Jenson and the man draped across his shoulder was Hiram.

'Holy shit, what happened?'

'I'll explain on the way, just get him in and drive!'

They heaved Hiram into the back passenger seat and buckled the seatbelt before slamming the doors and leaving in a screech of rubber and exhaust smoke onto the street. Jenson looked behind him to see the hotel staff standing in disbelief at what they had just witnessed.

'You realise the local cops are now probably after us!'

'Even more reason to get to the airport ASAP,' Jenson replied.

The diesel engine churned through the gears as they weaved through the thick Athens traffic on the way to the airfield. Jenson was flung across the back seats as they careered through a tight corner and onto the freeway. Hiram sat expressionless beside him despite the commotion of the situation. He looked just like any other commuter on a train or bus on their way to work on a Monday morning, looking demoralised and eager to be anywhere but here.

Abel had organised the jet to be ready and waiting at 9.30 a.m. He was already there, organising the process of exfiltration. They would need to be up in the air as soon as they could now the local police were on their tails, let alone the rebels from Istanbul.

Once on the freeway, they were able to blend in a little more and slowed the pace down to avoid attracting attention to themselves. Thankfully, they were able to access the private airfield away from the main entrance of the airport where a heavy security presence had been alerted to the situation. The black van rolled in next to the jet where Abel was standing, his black tie flapping in the breeze from the engines. Jenson got out and raced around to the other side of the vehicle to extract the lifeless Hiram from the passenger seat. Abel's face quickly turned to one of disbelief as he saw his boss slung over Jenson's shoulder.

'What the fuck happened?'

It was the first time Jenson had heard the man swear the entire time they had been working together.

'Not now. We need to get into the air ASAP.'

The stunned look on Abel's face remained as he climbed the stairs behind Jenson and Hiram, whose arms dangled precariously over the banister rails on the way up to the cabin. The awkward look across the crew's faces mimicked that of Abel; however, they dared not ask for fear of breaching their security clearance. They seemed to be sworn to secrecy as to what any of their plans had been over the past months and purely fulfilled theirs blissfully, unaware that they had been helping solve the world's most preeminent concern. Jenson found it hard to believe they were completely oblivious, though. The looks on their faces often showed signs of a knowing smirk and words were somehow spoken telepathically.

Jenson placed Hiram into a chair as gracefully as he could and shouted at the cabin crew to get going. The pilot kicked the engines into gear and swung the jet around for take-off. They were evidently dealing with the best in the business. The flashing lights of emergency vehicles could be seen from the freeway outside the airport. Their luminescent red and blue flashes pulsated through the glass into Jenson's eyes, creating a sense of panic he had not felt since escaping the hippo in the Congo with Kofi.

'Let's go! Let's go!' he screamed again.

There was no response from the pilot other than the radio transmission of their intention for take-off. Surely, they couldn't be stopped now, Jenson hoped. With that thought, the jet engines roared into action and he was jolted back into his backrest with the acceleration. They were airborne in a matter of seconds, looking at the ensuing chaos below unravel before them. Speeding police cars screeched around corners into the private airfield but it was too late.

Jenson took a long deep breath with the relief that they would not have to face another day under the attack of rebels or insulted governments. The issue at the hotel would resolve itself in time when the truth came out. He was confident there would be no consequences as a result of that, other than being refused entry at the hotel again, perhaps. The more pressing concern was the Turkish government and the fallout from their meeting that was cut short by protestors. He sank his head into his palms and tried not to think about it too much for now. They were heading home, at last, and he was eager to get some normality back into his life. He looked over at Hiram and feared that he would end up just like him if he kept this up.

'Here you go, sir.' The solitary crew member outside of the flight staff stood next to Jenson with a tumbler of whiskey. 'Your favourite. No ice, just how you like it.'

He accepted the offering and looked up at the kind face standing before him. 'Thank you.'

'You're most welcome.'

'Hey,' he interrupted before she went back to the cockpit. 'Isn't it ten in the morning?'

'Not where we're going.' She smiled. 'You deserve it either way.'

He rose the glass in the air and took a sip of the golden liquid. The silky, soft, warming glow slid down his throat and into his stomach. It was exactly what he needed. He rested his head on the back of the seat and tried not to think about Hiram, who was sitting across the aisle from him, mute and lifeless yet again. At least they had a protocol in place for situations such as this. Nya's intuition to treat him in the method that she had the first time around had really been the catalyst for implementing their findings in the field. What intrigued Jenson now was why some people, such as Hiram, clearly seemed to be more susceptible to SK01 than others. They had both been exposed to the same levels of anthropomorphic factors over the past few months, yet Hiram seemed to be far more sensitive to its effects than him. He sipped at the glass again and closed his eyes.

Something for another day, he thought. Not long afterwards, the heavy weight of fatigue took over and he was asleep. The white noise of the engine proved to be the perfect thing to numb his racing mind; perhaps the morning glass of whisky helped as well.

CHAPTER 43

THREE MONTHS LATER

The river eddied in and out of the rocks and around Jenson's ankles, his waders insulating his feet against the chill of the mountain water. He cast the fly into a calm section of water where a few riverbank gums provided protection for the brown trout that called this stretch of water home. All that could be heard above the rush of the river was the echo of whip birds and currawongs. The sun was getting low in the sky and the grove of mountain ash glowed as it descended towards the horizon for another day. It was days like this that Jenson loved most about living at Capertree. The simplicity of life never seemed dull; it just was. After months of being transported across the globe, he appreciated staying in the one place for a while. He'd even taken some time away from work to get into the groove. The lingering fear of SK01 was also present and he thought it a sensible move to practice what he preached.

It was then he heard the crunching sound of gravel from up near the house. It was closely followed by the slam of a car door and footsteps up onto the timber veranda of his house. It was rare to get visitors; Jenson could count on one hand the number of people who knew exactly where he lived. That was exactly the way he liked it. He set the fly in the same place, trying not to be distracted by an unwelcome visitor but as he slowly reeled it in, he saw a man perched up on the bank. He knew exactly who those unwavering eyes and tall stance belonged to.

'Any luck?'

'Not with you standing on the bank throwing a shadow into my cast,' he replied, not even looking up from his gaze at the water.

Hiram stepped down from the riverbank and met Jenson by the edge to shake his hand.

'It's nice to see you up and on your feet again. You look far better than the last time I saw you.' Jenson removed the fly and placed it in his vest pocket.

'I feel it too,' Hiram replied as he followed Jenson up the bank and to the house.

'Fancy a drink?'

'Should I be worried, considering the last time I had one with you I ended up incapacitated?'

'You think this has all been my doing?' Jenson replied with a smile. He reached into a wooden cupboard and retrieved two whisky tumblers and a bottle of Scotch.

'Just a suggestion. I can't claim to have done any significant research on the hypothesis.'

'You should probably drink your drink then,' Jenson said as he handed him the glass. 'You've come a long way to say hello and prove to me that you're healthy again.'

Hiram paused and looked sheepishly up at Jenson, who was standing by the fire. 'You're right,' he finally said. 'I came to offer you a job.'

'With CINS?'

Hiram nodded. 'You know our people, how we work and what we do. And we can trust you. Plus, you're not bad at what you do.'

'The highest praise coming from you.' The fire cracked as he stoked another log and shut the door. The smell of wood smoke that filled the room combined with the whisky seemed to relax them both. 'You realise I have a job, right?'

'I do. But I think your skill set is perfect for what we need and we can provide you with the resources and autonomy you need to pursue what interests you.'

It did sound enticing but Jenson had built his reputation as a researcher, not a government employee extinguishing spot fires. Albeit, SK01 was more of a catastrophic blaze than a spot fire. Plus, he didn't want to seem too eager straight off the bat. There was something to be said for playing hard to get in situations such as this.

Hiram could sense the hesitation in Jenson's body language and proceeded to list off the portfolios he would manage and the team he would have at his disposal. It included Nya and Emerson, which pleased him.

'You all worked so well together. I thought, why not keep a winning team together to solve the rest of the world's problems?'

Jenson smiled as he stared out the window at the dense green foliage and orange glow of the sunset. The satisfaction he gained from working on the SK01 case was immense, he couldn't doubt that. Since they had returned to HQ, the scale of the problem had been de-escalated from a state of emergency and was now in the hands of respective governments to manage. Somehow a small group of people from an eclectic background of professions had managed to collaborate and solve the mystery. In the process, they had cast a light on the current state of human wellbeing worldwide. The identification of SK01 had created an awareness of how humans were living and the findings proved to be stark and unflattering. Jenson had been asked for interviews from just about every news station on the planet, a request he now politely declined. In every one of them, he made a point to highlight the root cause of SK01. Homo sapiens evolved to move, innovate and utilise their mental and physical prowess for the sake of survival across millennia. What the team at CINS had succeeded in highlighting was just how far removed modern human beings had diverged from that core principle. Not only was the health of the planet being jeopardised from human activity, their own health was as well.

'For years, we have focused on the physical decline in human health due to the anthropomorphic shift on planet Earth,' Jenson had said in one interview. 'But what we now understand is the human mind is just as sensitive to the requirements of our evolutionary past.'

Hiram broke Jenson's train of deep thought as he placed a hand on his shoulder.

'Have a think about it. You know where to find me,' he said as he went to walk out the door, the soles of his dress shoes knocking on the wooden floorboards. Jenson replied with a nod and a smile. Somehow, he already knew the answer. He suspected Hiram did too.

'Oh, one other thing.' Hiram stopped in the doorway and pulled out an envelope from his jacket pocket. 'We received your mail while you were away, for the sake of confidentiality. You received most of it when we first returned but it appears this one got lost amongst the pile.'

'You went through my mail?' Jenson protested as he reached out and grabbed the envelope.

'You were fully aware we'd take measures such as that. You didn't even have your phone or access to personal email the entire time we were working on the case.' There was a long pause before Jenson looked up from his observation of the handwriting on the envelope.

'Don't have much to hide anyway.'

Hiram nodded with a knowing look. 'I'll speak to you soon. Don't take too long to decide whether you're coming over to the best in the business.'

'Sure thing, boss.'

Jenson stood in the doorway of his house and watched the red taillights of Hiram's car drift out of view until all he could hear once again was the trickle of the river and the final birdsong of the evening; a crackle from the fire finally broke him from his daydream. He closed the door behind him and set the note on the kitchen bench. He knew that writing so well it had taken less than a second before he registered who it was from and why it had been held onto by CINS.

Sasha had been ill since SK01 became a classified disease state, even before Jenson had been recruited by CINS. He'd received several voicemails from her in the time he was away. They followed the typical course of someone experiencing the crippling effects of SK01. Despair, confusion and pain were riddled through a scramble of lucid messages. As she had said herself numerous times, she had no idea why she was calling Jenson or what prompted her to call. She just had a gut feeling. It was only later that she had seen her ex-husband on television talking about the illness and part of it started to make sense.

Jenson sat down and looked at the envelope, wondering whether he should open it all. He had left that life behind and was happy in a place where they had decided Sasha wouldn't be. Fidgeting with the glass in his hands, he opened his laptop on the bench nearby. He opened a web browser and began searching for flights to the Congo and Greenland. Maybe he'd go to one from the other. Maybe he would go to one and come home for a while. All he knew was that he needed to go back and see Kofi and Wolff. There needed to be some closure. The glow of the laptop screen disappeared as he shut the lid and sat back in his chair. The warmth from the fire made him sleepy along with the dimming light that filtered through the windows. Moonlight had taken over from the sun and all that illuminated the inside of the house was a solitary globe and the fire. A silence around the landscape ensued as the transition from day to night took place. The pace of the world seemed to slow temporarily, the only constant remained the river quietly running, creating its own path, however long it would take.

Shawline Publishing Group Pty Ltd
www.shawlinepublishing.com.au

More great Shawline titles can be found here:

New titles also available through Books@Home Pty Ltd.
Subscribe today - www.booksathome.com.au